# Abhorrent
# Faith

## john baltisberger

St. Rooster Books

Published by St. Rooster Books.
ISBN: 978-1-955745-09-3

First Edition
Contact St. Rooster Book at Tim-Murr @ live . com

John Baltisberger

# Praise for the Abhorrent Series

*"An unwholesome and unholy blend of body horror and biblical wrath, Baltisberger unleashes the anger seething just beneath the surface of the sacred, unveiling the profane"*
**– Nik Robinson, author of You Will Be Consumed**

+

*"Baltisberger creates something truly extraordinary here. In a pressure cooker setting, an incendiary interfaith debate literally transforms into monstrous physical and carnal combat."* -- **The Professor, Author of Ejaculate of the Incubus**

+

*"Abhorrent Faith, the second part of Baltisberger's Abhorrent series, is phenomenal. Baltisberger really shows his range with this book and demonstrates why he is a top contender in the world of horror fiction."* — **Daniel Volpe, author of Gift of Death and Left to You**

+

*"A great big gory extravaganza!"* – **Edward Lee, author of City Infernal and White Trash Gothic**

+

*"Adapting unnatural ideas into a twisted mass of contorted images is an obvious strength of Baltisberger. His ingredients of bile, bone and viscera make up a recipe specifically geared towards a baked gore platter served on each and every page."* - **Mike Rankin, Horror Bookworm Reviews**

This book is dedicated to the diligent person who called 911 when someone set fire to my synagogue.

This book is dedicated to the kind community and people who donated to repair the damages.

This book is dedicated to anyone who stands up against bigotry and hate.

# Chapter 1

"I just think that it's disgusting that people, because they don't want to offend anyone, would offend the one who died for their sins."

It was shouted out, complete with a fist banging against the table, shaking the cutlery and dishes. Everyone in the room was silent for several moments before the assembled clergy burst into laughter. Seated around the small table, a handful of the religious leaders of San Antonio, Texas was gathered for their monthly interfaith dinner.

"No, I'm serious!" Dan Parter objected to the laughter. "That's what my grandmother told me!"

"Where is she from again?" asked Rabbi Ari Goldberg, his hand resting on his wife Sarah's knee next to him.

"The Middle Ages," answered Madri Nambiyar, one of the local pandits. She was busy pulling her own dishes for the potluck out of a small bag. She generally brought the best dishes.

"No, she was from Crisp, which just feels like it's stuck in the Middle Ages," Dan objected with mock outrage.

"Not everyone here knows the back roads of Texas, Dan; you might want to tell someone that Crisp isn't on the outskirts of Hell," Father Jeremy Fennec teased, though he looked a little distraught at the sight of all the vegetarian dishes being pulled out and set on the table.

"We've all been to Dallas, I'm sure," Muneed al-Saab interjected before Dan could argue about the proximity of Hell to Texas and vice versa.

The seven of them were only a small segment of the interfaith community and team, but during a breakout session at a retreat, they had found common ground, friendship, and decided to keep that going. They rotated locations and days — while a Sunday wasn't a particularly great day for the Christians, as clergy, all of them were mostly busy every day of the week, so it was only fair that the pastor and priest join the group this Sunday evening. Gathering for an early dinner once a month with varied voices across the city of people who wanted to help, who wanted to do something to help those in need, was as much food for the gathered individuals as the actual food.

Eventually, everything was on the table, and the pitchers of ice tea, sweet and unsweetened, made it around the table. Everyone found their seats and then looked towards Ari to lead a blessing. It was just a simple formality, they were all people of faith, and it had been decided that whoever was hosting would lead the blessing. Ari tended to go with something more humanist, more universal than religious, it just seemed appropriate for what they were all trying to accomplish.

"I am grateful to be here with my friends, in good health, with good food. I am hopeful that the people of our world who suffer under the weight of intolerance will take our example and grow, and hopeful that through loving kindness, we are able to effect tikkun olam, a healing of this world."

"Amen!" Father Fennec agreed, pouring himself a glass of sweet tea. He paused when he saw Madri looking pointedly at the casserole dish he had brought.

"And that is?" she asked.

"Uh, that would be macaroni and cheese."

"With …" Muneed pressed.

"Bacon …" Fennec admitted. "I'm sorry, I forgot that bacon is pork. You know, I think of pork chops and ham, I don't think about the other stuff."

Dan rolled his eyes but smiled. "You also seem to forget that we try to keep it vegetarian," he chided as he scooped a spoonful of the non-kosher dish onto his plate. "Hopefully, Rabbi Ari has a lesson in mindfulness for us today."

Dan was a lanky man. He had served in the military for a bit, a combat medic in the US Army, did three tours of duty in Afghanistan before an IED had given him the gift of chronic pain, a limp, and an honorable discharge. Unsure where else to go, Dan had gone to seminary, much to his folks' delight. Much to their horror, it had been Methodist and not Baptist. He just didn't have the fire, brimstone, and bigotry required to be the sort of man his family wished he was. Of course, no one here was that sort of person, that sort of fear-mongering, close-minded bigotry that his family delighted in would never join the table at an interfaith committee.

Serving himself a large plate of saag paneer, Patrick Howards, the president of one of the local Buddhist temples, shrugged a little. "It happens, we all make mistakes. And that just leaves more delicious options for those of us who abstain from meat and pork." He was a washed-up Californian, a former competitive surfer who had given up everything after his longtime boyfriend had died, and had found solace in the tenets of Buddhism. "Unless Ari would rather not have pork in the synagogue at all," he quickly added.

Ari waved it away. "A lot of my congregants don't keep kosher, but for future reference, I would prefer you didn't bring pork. Just out of respect for those who do."

Father Fennec held his hands up in surrender, chastised. "Changing the subject entirely, how are y'all's food drives going?"

Dan rolled his eyes and sighed. "Not fantastic, people keep trying to bring in cans for the drive. I keep telling them we need donations of money for the food bank not actual food."

"It's hard for people to break habits, especially when you have an older congregation," Madri suggested.

From there, the talking broke down to individual conversations, checking in on current events and how things were going in each other's personal lives. Carefully avoiding the topic of politics. There would be time for that afterwards if anyone wanted to, after the talk Rabbi Ari had planned. But they were only a few minutes into their dinner when an older man entered the public room and approached the table. Ari stood at his approach.

"Uh, everyone, this is Jose Martinez, he's our building manager." Like most synagogues, Congregation Beth Shalom hired non-Jewish workers who could work on Shabbot without worrying about religious law. Jose worked on Saturday and took other days he wanted off. "Hey, Jose, what's up?"

Jose nodded to the other religious leaders, wringing his hands a bit, betraying his nervous feelings. "Sorry to interrupt, Rabbi, but I was watching the news, and there are riots breaking out all over Texas right now, and there have been a lot of reports of violence in this area. I'm going to go lock and chain all the doors, just until it calms down, or when the parents come to get their kids." He was referring to the day care and religious school kids who came to Shul on Sunday evenings to learn Hebrew and Torah. They were upstairs at the moment.

Ari looked around the table at the others and slowly nodded. "Yeah, of course, if any of you want to head out early ... get home?" He paused, his mouth unable to keep up with his racing thoughts. Why were there riots? And all over Texas? He prided himself in keeping up with current events, but he hadn't heard any noises about any demonstrations or rallies that could set off riots being planned. "We can always do a rain check."

Jose waited a moment, just to make sure no one wanted to get out before he locked up, but when no one stood, he turned and left to secure the building.

After Jose left, the table erupted into conversation, each person trying to guess what could be causing unrest.

"Texas is becoming quite the hot spot for this sort of thing," Madri said with a knowing nod.

"Well, it only goes to show, Texas is becoming more and more blue as time passes, it brings a lot of tension with the red roots and the government,"

Patrick agreed

"If Texas is so blue, why the hell are we still electing all of these republican senators and governors?" Fennec argued. "Seems to me that despite the influx of Californians bringing the liberal agenda to the state, things remain pretty solidly red."

"Then you aren't paying attention," Dan said after he finished swallowing. "What you have to remember, Jeremy, is that at the end of the day, the Republicans who were running things saw the writing on the wall, so they gerrymandered the entire state to the point that no matter how people in the cities where all these Californians and younger people live, it's the older, wealthier, and whiter population that retains the power." Dan shrugged. "Doesn't matter what your political bent is, it's pretty common knowledge that's how politicians stay in power." He sighed a little, reached into his pocket to grab a prescription bottle, and popped two pills in his mouth, then washed them down with sweet tea.

"Well sure," Jeremy admitted. "But we have to deal with whoever is in power, and we have to work together with everyone, both sides of the aisle, in order to get things done."

Madri nodded. "I don't think anyone was suggesting that we not work with someone due to their politics."

"There's this story I really like," Ari began, "where this rabbi sees a sick man go into a temple dedicated to Aesculapius, the Roman god of healing, and he comes out healthy. The rabbi, frustrated at this, knowing it will lead Jews to abandon their faith in favor of this other god, asks, 'God, why are you allowing these people to be healed in the temples of our oppressors?' And God answered, because in these stories, God is far more vocal than in most of our experiences, 'Should I withhold the appointed time of healing simply because they are in the wrong place?'"

Ari paused to take a bite before gesturing with his fork. "I like that story a lot, and I think it's especially important now, right? It doesn't matter if we agree with people or not, we have to try to heal and to help. We have to meet people where they are, not where we wish they would be. Our jobs have to be to move the state further towards being in line with loving kindness, even if that seems impossible sometimes."

"But," argued Muneed, "if we are providing aid to people who are in turn oppressing others, or if we assist someone in need who then takes their newfound position to harm others, aren't we complicit in that harm or oppression?"

"Hmm, I disagree, Muneed," Sarah said. "I think that reflects on them, not us. I know," she raised her hands as if to defend her position, "that's not a popular position, especially now; but I think that's because we're all stuck in a macro view of things. Look more into the micro again. If you pass by a homeless man and you give him money, is it possible that he's going to buy drugs? Yes. Is it possible that they aren't actually homeless, that it's a scam? Yes. But it's also possible that neither of those things is true. Sure, my ten dollars here and there isn't going to address the big issues, the homelessness, the addiction, it won't change gentrification or housing costs, it won't get them psychiatric help."

"But they will have the option to eat, we'll have eased their suffering, just a bit," Dan finished for her. "But we can't just focus on the micro, Sarah, because we are the next step up. We have to lobby for better laws, we have to petition our government for better funding for public health and addiction programs. We have to be the ones who are partnering with housing projects and building affordable housing. And to Muneed's point, if we are partnering or giving our time, energy, and money to politicians and groups who don't support those humanitarian efforts, we're actively working against our stated purpose. You know, I hate to say it, but helping everyone at once isn't possible until those groups stop fighting each other."

"Well, I think part of the problem is with corporations trying to enforce their theological views on their employees and customers," Jeremy said. "Christianity in particular is supposed to be a personal religion. Whenever you try to bring it to a culture, it begins to get oppressive. I think any faith would, right? People always point at Islam, but we have some pretty oppressive little Christian groups right here in America too. I don't know how it is with Judaism or Buddhism, but—"

"It's the same. No matter what religion you look at, you'll find abuse of it somewhere," Dan cut in. "I understand where you're coming from, Muneed, and I get what you're saying, Sarah, but we can't afford to ever paint anything as black and white, we have to look at everything as nuanced."

He was about to go on when the crash of breaking glass followed by a terrifying scream startled him into silence. From somewhere near the front of the synagogue, the sound of tearing and bestial grunts could be heard. Everyone froze, eyes wide, staring towards the door of the auditorium, where they had been eating.

"Sarah," Ari whispered, "go upstairs and help with the kids, keep everyone quiet. I'll come get you when it's safe."

Sarah looked like she would argue for a moment; she didn't want to get up, she didn't want to risk traveling through the synagogue alone. But she couldn't leave the children and the young college student who was teaching them on their own either. She nodded and rose, walking quickly at first before breaking into a jog to reach the back doors of the auditorium.

As soon as she was gone, Ari rose. "I'll go check it out."

"Not alone you won't," Dan muttered, rising as well, along with Jeremy. "Jeremy, sit down, someone needs to stay here with the …" he trailed off.

"With the defenseless women?" Muneed finished for him. Dan had the good grace to blush. "Go, the two of you can check out the scary noise; we'll wait here." She smiled, putting on a brave face to hide the fear she felt. They all understood that in today's world, the chances of some monster using a riot as an excuse to break into a synagogue to hurt the people inside was all too realistic.

"Quick question, though; what are you going to do if someone is coming in with a gun or a knife?" Patrick asked.

"Jose keeps a gun in his office," Ari explained. "If need be, I can run and grab it; but hopefully, it's just someone throwing rocks and it won't escalate beyond that."

"And those sounds?" Madri asked.

They all fell silent for a moment, listening. From the auditorium, it was impossible to tell what was happening outside. They all heard the grotesque tearing sounds and the growls, but identifying them was beyond any of the assembled clergy.

"We'll check it out," Ari said finally, somewhat sheepishly. "I'm sure it will be okay." He said it with more confidence than he felt, but he pushed on regardless. He started off towards the front doors of the auditorium, walking a little slower so Dan, with his limp, could keep up.

"What are we actually going to do if there's someone dangerous in here?" Dan asked as he caught up. "Ask him to wait patiently while you run to Jose's office to find a gun?"

Ari shook his head. "No, look, it won't come to that. Most people, when confronted by the people they think they want to hurt, they lose the stomach for it; we'll go out there, find a vandal who will run as soon as he sees that people are here." Ari stopped in his tracks as the double doors to the auditorium swung open.

A man stood there. He was disheveled and bloody, his arms hung at his side, and in his right hand, gripped by curly black hair, was Jose's head, ripped from its shoulders, staring with terrified dead eyes at the rabbi.

+

It took several seconds before the assembled members of the interfaith dinner group could figure out what was happening. They saw the disheveled man, the way his muscles seemed to twitch and squirm under his skin. They saw his bloodshot eyes, which seemed to glow with a reddish pulse under the mop of ragged, stringy black hair. They saw that in his hand, his misshapen hand with more digits than it should have, he was clutching the severed head of the building manager, saw the blood that dripped from the ragged stump of his neck and the horrific vision of the shorn bit of spine that dangled from the skull. For a moment, no one moved.

Madri was the first to react, rising from her seat and dashing in the opposite direction. Her sudden dash for freedom broke the spell, and someone screamed. The man, who had been still after entering, moved, he moved faster than anyone ought to be able to move, his legs propelling him across the room. At the last second before he reached Madri, he leapt in the air and brought Jose's head down on hers with a sickening crack. The rest of them rose; Jeremy, Muneed, and Patrick moved forward, hoping to pull the madman off Madri.

Despite their best intentions, they were far too late. Jose's skull had crushed in Madri's head. Her nose caved in, crumpling down into her brain, the skin tearing like cellophane stretched over the jagged bits of broken skull. Her scream was short, a bark of sonic noise before it was broken off along with her tongue in the blunt force trauma done to her face. Bits of flesh and teeth flew in every direction from the strength with which the man was hammering it down into her. Blood geysered from the shredded meat of her face, her features were obliterated. Skull fragments and one eye lay on the floor next to her corpse as the man frantically continued to pound his hands into the wet meat of her brains.

Patrick tackled the man off of Madri's corpse. The two rolled a few feet, but the man ended on top. He let loose a horrifying discordant scream and bent down, biting into Patrick's face. The man's teeth, jagged and uneven, tore into Patrick's eye and cheek. The Buddhist's screams mingled with the man's warbled cries as he swallowed and bent down to bite again. Bits of the Patrick's face dangled from the man's mouth, and under the monster, the man writhed, though his struggling was getting weaker by the second.

Muneed grabbed one of the chairs that was scattered around the auditorium and swung it at the madman as hard as she could. The twitching murderer howled in rage as he was knocked clear of his new meal. The man turned towards Muneed and bellowed, blood flecked drool flying from his mouth, jaw unhinged and stretched wide, as he unleashed his discordant scream. Muneed, still operating on adrenaline, roared back and charged, swinging the folding chair like a mace, trying to drive the monster back so that Jeremy could reach Patrick and save him.

Muneed kept advancing. She was not a violent woman, but the sight of her friends hurt, the terror of the man's misshapen appearance drove her on to attack the madman. The thing, it couldn't really be called a man anymore, slid back, avoiding Muneed's clumsy attacks easily, hissing with each step. Muneed, perhaps overconfident because of her weapon, charged, shouting, but the man dodged under her chair, moving faster than Muneed could follow, and swiped at Muneed with fingers that had fused together into one big powerful digit tipped with a dripping claw. Muneed dropped like a brick, clutching her stomach, her eyes wide with shock and fear.

The creature launched itself past Muneed's collapsed form and tore through the carpeted auditorium, howling as it launched itself at Jeremy. Jeremy shouted and raised his hands, trying to fend off the thing's assault. That vicious claw swung, severing Jeremy's arm at the elbow and sending it flying across the room to land among the bacon mac n' cheese. It wasn't a clean sever either; the skin was shredded, and muscle hung from the dripping wound. The bone jutted from the mass of ragged muscle, fractured and shorn by the impact. Jeremy's scream of pain was cut off as the creature whipped its arm back around in the other direction and slammed it into Jeremy's shoulder, forcing him to his knees with a cry of pain. Unable to catch himself, Jeremy collapsed into a quivering pile, desperately clutching at the stump where his arm used to be.

The monster blinked its eyes; there were five of them now. Had there been five when the man had first come in? There were five now, each one swiveling madly as the creature sought its next target, the next person that presented itself as a threat. They landed on Ari one at a time, disjointed and then suddenly in sync as the creature gathered itself to leap and tear into another victim.

"Down!" a commanding voice called from

behind Ari, from the doorway.

The creature, the thing that had been a man at some point, whined and sank back on its haunches, offering no argument to the command. Dan, who had taken a few steps towards Ari, turned to look at this new voice. Standing in the doorway was a small older man; he wore a faded and threadbare suit and carried a large gold leaf bible in one hand. His skin was the horrible off-orange of spray tan and looked clammy, his hair was a greasy salt-and-pepper that clung to his scalp. The worst was his face, which was situated on an over-sized head for his small frame. He looked like someone had modeled a human face on a skull from description only, as though they had never seen an actual human face. His eyes were bulging orbs that sat deep in the sockets, wild and insane. His thin lips curled back from his short ugly teeth in what looked more like a snarl than a smile.

He took a step forward and raised his empty hand like he was addressing the nation. "Heel!"

The assembled clergy watched in stunned silence as the bloody monstrosity heeded this new preacher and loped to his side and sat on its haunches like a loyal hound.

Ari took a step towards Muneed, who was mewling in pain, her intestines slipping in her hands.

"Hold on, ain't no one told you to move," the newcomer barked. "You stay right where you are."

Dan looked between the man and Muneed. "You gotta let me take care of her. She's hurt; she's going to die without medical attention." He paused and then pointed at where Jeremy lay, pale as the white tiles above them, trying to stop the blood. "And him too. They need help."

"Now, why would I let you take care of her, a towel-head whore? Or him, for that matter? I see that collar. The Catholic church ain't nothing but a gang of pedophiles and sodomites. I got a better question, though; why would any truly god-fearing man be caught breaking bread with the likes of Christ's murderers?" He looked around the room at the bodies of dead that lay in messy broken piles. "Christ-killers and heathens. That's bad company there."

"I'm going to help her," Dan said through tight lips. He didn't know who this fucker was, but he knew the kind of language he was throwing around. Southern Baptist hate monger, Dan was fluent in it, no matter how much he wished he could wash that part of his past away. He didn't know what else to say. Who was this man? How was he controlling that thing? And what the goddamned fuck was that thing? He walked towards Muneed, waiting for the hateful pastor to sick his … his … monster on him.

Ari watched Dan move away and then turned back towards the man. "I don't know what's happening, but whatever it is—"

"It would be obvious to any true man of God, rabbi, it would be very clear." The man, the preacher, walked casually up to the table and picked up Jeremy's arm. He glanced at it, licking his lips hungrily before shaking his head and tossing it aside haphazardly, then dug his free hand into the mac n cheese to take a bite. Around his mouthfuls of swine and carbs, he spoke.

"The people riot, and it is the worst in places thick with homos and junkies. The spiritually poor who ignored all of Jesus's calls to service have begun to labor under the mark. Those who gave in to the commies and faeries, those who delighted at promiscuity. It is all happening as John the Revelator once wrote. The apocalypse is come, and the beast walks the earth."

# Chapter 2

Ari stared at the intruder; if not for the dead and dying in the room, he may have laughed. But seeing this madman, and whatever it was that had killed Madri and Jose, Ari could barely get his thoughts collected.

"What? The apocalypse? The beast?" Ari asked, trying to find some sort of rock he could cling to in the deluge of madness that had been unleashed on his little synagogue this evening.

The preacher turned to face him and smiled; his teeth were yellow, and several were capped in gold. It wasn't a pleasant smile. It was the kind of smile that promised pain. These kinds of smiles had been used for as long as humanity had existed. They graced the faces of abusive husbands, corrupt cops, and power-hungry clergy, each with the same promise of cruel control. "I should introduce myself. My name is Pastor Aiden King, and I come bearing the good news."

Ari wanted to shut the man up, to tell him to shove his good news up his ass, but he couldn't; so long as the man was proselytizing, he wasn't stopping Dan from helping Muneed. He looked between King and the monstrous twitching man beside him, which was looking more and more horrifying as time passed. His jaw, which had unhinged at one point, hung loose and low, wobbling with every spasm. The mouth that was revealed was completely filled with rows of jagged teeth, so many teeth at so many angles that Ari was sure the man would never be able to close his mouth again. A wheezing whine emerged from the cavernous maw with every breath, as though the changes inside the man were as terrible and malformed as those that were visible. The bulbous eyes, which seemed to multiply even as Ari watched, blinked and pulsed with an evil red glow, giving the already demonic looking creature a further diabolic air.

"Ah, and this is brother Joseph Moore." King rested a hand on the shoulder of the killer. "He's a member of my flock. I brought him along with me today to make sure we would be able to accomplish our holy mission."

"Holy miss—" Ari began and then stopped himself. "You brought him here? He killed people, he murdered two people, maybe more." Ari gestured to where Dan sat with Muneed, trying to help her hold her intestines in, trying to wrap her up.

+

"Shh," Dan whispered to Muneed, "it's going to be okay. I know it looks scary, but you're intact, nothing internal is ripped. I've seen soldiers survive wounds like this," he lied. He knew her time was limited; even in the best of scenarios, your organs should be inside your body.

Muneed choked back a bitter, pained laugh. She was slipping into delirium, unable to focus well. "You have? Where?"

"In Afgh—" He frowned and looked down, focusing back on his work. The truth was that he had spent most of his youth trying to shoot and kill Muslims like her. He had been pointed by Uncle Sam at brown people on another continent and told it was us or them. It had taken a lot of long nights, therapy, and drinks to overcome the prejudice that his family and too many of his fellow soldiers had planted deep into his psyche. "While I was in the army," he finished.

He pulled off his overshirt and pushed it against her wound, trying to stem the flow of blood. She already looked waxy and pallid. With his free hand, he reached down and gently began trying to feed her intestines back through the open wound in her stomach. The long ropes of her guts were slippery and dark, like Vaseline coated serpents that slid between his fingers as he tried to help her without looking. He didn't smell feces, which meant her intestines hadn't ruptured ... or maybe the smell of blood was too overpowering. It was everywhere, overpowering, combined with the feeling of her intestines in his hand, it was all he could do not to vomit. He worked her entrails back into her abdomen and pulled his shirt around her midsection, tying it as tight as he dared, hoping it would be enough to retard the blood flow and keep her insides inside of her.

He fished into his pocket and pulled out a prescription bottle. He rattled it around and pushed it open. "Here ... take these." He shook four pills out; it was too much, an overdose at this strength. But he didn't want her to be in pain, and maybe this would help her.

Muneed weakly pushed at his hand. "What is it?"

"Hydrocodone, I take it for my injury; it's just going to help with the pain, make it bearable, that's all," Dan answered. He needed to get her calm and as stable as he could so he could check on Jeremy.

Muneed resisted another moment, then a tremor of pain shook her body and she relented, allowing him to bring the pills to her mouth and swallowing painfully.

"Okay, I'll be right back. I'm going to check on Jeremy." He stood, thankful that Ari was engaging the lunatic and monster, giving him the time he needed to help the priest.

+

"He wanted to make sure everyone stayed in one place, that's what I asked him to do, and he did make sure that happened," King was saying, stroking the top of Joseph Moore's head as though the deformed creature was some sort of loyal hound.

"What? Why? Why would you do this? What is

he?" Ari sputtered as he spoke, trying to wrap his mind around the foul and disturbing evening.

"He's a man, a lost man. His name is Joseph. And he is struggling, dying under the weight of the mark." King looked up. "Look at him, rabbi, look at how the man suffers and changes, twisted into some demonic thing by the power of the Antichrist. Scripture warns that the world will be drowned in blood, and the first blood will be that of the heathens and apostates." He gestured to the body of Madri and to where Muneed lay taking quick shallow breaths. "He could sense that they were not godly, and his mission, no, his very blood calls to purge the world of the unclean."

It was only years of experience in dealing with the ignorant that stopped Ari from blurting out that it was 2025 and it was long past time for the ideology of *unclean* people to be done away with. He pressed his lips together in a tight line. The pastor had already said how he felt about Jews; Christ-killer, he had called him. Which only begged the question …

"Why did you stop him from killing me then? How did you stop him?" Ari asked.

"How? The mark has no power over the faithful.

In Christ, I am saved and protected and given dominion over all things on this earth, especially over junkies and whores. Joseph here is a heroin junkie, or he was. Now he is a damned thing, but he is working for God's glory, as all things do. Earning his salvation one drop of heathen blood at a time." King paused shaking his head. "How wondrous is God that I was able to throw off the shackles of addiction, become clean in body as well as in his eyes. That I am now given control over the beasts that spread under the shadow of the Antichrist. This power is also a commandment, a mission from God Almighty. I have been denied the rapture and been given the gift of service in Jesus Christ's name, Amen!"

"So, you're going around murdering non-Christians," Ari said, overcome by the horror of what he was seeing and hearing. How did the rational mind deal with the impossibility that sat in front of him?

"No, I am cleansing our world of those who would deny Christ and serve Satan! I am cleansing and I am saving!" King roared, his eyes blazing with the same terrible red light that was bleeding from Joseph Moore. King cleared his throat and shook his head, twitching as though pushing back against some baser, violent instinct.

"The scripture says that Jesus will come back, Jesus will come back when the Jews, his murders, convert to his fellowship or return to Israel and flood the land with their blood. One is easier, but it would be a grave injustice, it would be an unconscionable evil to not try to save the souls of those chosen. What greater stick in the devil's eye than bringing the truth of salvation to those who murdered Jesus himself. That, my fallen friend, is why I am here."

+

Dan wasn't paying attention to the conversation — or rather, the monologue — going on. He hurried to Jeremy's side, removing his belt as he walked. Jeremy had lost a lot of blood, but he had done the best he could to stem the flow, pushing himself back against one of the room's support pillars and clamping his remaining hand over the wound. The wound was terrible, but at least this was one that people survived. This was something Dan could help with.

"Hey, Father Fennec," Dan said as he crouched down next to the injured man. "How you holding up?"

"Oh, you know, I've had better," he whispered with a pained smile. "Guess they're serious about not bringing pork inside."

Dan laughed at the terrible joke while he made a tourniquet of his belt and tightened it around Jeremy's arm. "Eye for an eye and arm for some bacon, that tracks." He kept his eyes on Jeremy's bicep, trying not to look down at the jagged bone and torn muscle that was visible through the shredded remains of Jeremy's shirt. Once the tourniquet was tight and not going anywhere, Dan looked back at Jeremy's face. The older priest was in pain, and honestly, the pain would only get worse until he slipped into shock, like poor Muneed.

Dan reached back into his pocket and pulled out his prescription bottle. "I'm going to give you a couple of hydrocodone, help take the edge off, okay?" He glanced down at the bottle, he only had 5 of the little pills left. Without them, he could barely function. The pain in his leg, coupled with the effects of withdrawal, was severe. But once this was over, once they got past this Pastor King and his monstrous attack dog … then he could refill his prescription, if the doctor would let him. Giving away 7 pills meant he would be out before his refill was ready. Dan stared down at the bottle. He could be without his hydrocodone for days, maybe longer, if he gave them away.

The hiss of pain from Jeremy brought Dan's attention back to the moment.

"I don't know, Dan, I have an addictive personality, any risk?"

Dan swallowed, he could almost feel himself breaking out in a cold sweat, but he smiled and shook his head.

"Nah, no real risk," he lied. Of course they were addictive as fuck, but also necessary, necessary to stop the pain, necessary to function, and despite his fear of running out, necessary to help Muneed and Jeremy. He quickly opened the bottle and tapped two pills out to hand to Jeremy. "They'll make you a little loopy if you're not used to them, but a little loopy in exchange for the pain should be a good deal."

Jeremy nodded. "Thank God for painkillers and doctors, huh?" He popped the two pills and swallowed like a champ before looking over Dan's shoulder to where the newcomer was shouting at

Ari. "What the hell is happening, Dan? How did this happen?"

Dan shook his head; he was just as clueless.

+

Ari was not clueless, though he would never give voice to it to his friends; this was the natural progression of Christian politics over the centuries. The Catholic church and the Protestants after them had fomented a war of propaganda and hate since the foundation of Paulian Christianity. Rumors of Blood Libel, charges of being Christ's murderers, accusations of using the blood of Christian infants to make Pesach bread. Even more open-minded and kind men like Dan and Jeremy taught that Pontius Pilate tried to free Jesus but the Jews refused. A millennia old tradition of exonerating the Roman oppressors and condemning the Jews. They still taught that the Saggacees, the rabbinic forefathers, were corrupt and evil, while history taught an entirely different truth.

Whether they wanted to admit it or not, Christian theology remained culpable in the anti-Semitic actions of the 21st century. From the gun threats to the Swastika banners that had been shown over the highway in Austin to the fires set outside of the synagogue just a few weeks back. They were all part of a war that Jews wanted no part in and Christians pretended wasn't on their shoulders. Pastor Aiden King was not the exception, he was the manifestation of all that hate given a voice.

Ari had been familiar with the old lines of antisemitism growing up, but being raised in a strong Jewish community, it had always seemed a distant specter, a looming boogeyman that was as much parable as reality. He always knew it existed, he had studied the history of hatred and had family who had escaped the Holocaust, as well as family who didn't. But when he came to Texas, his experience had changed. Instead of being surrounded by the familiar, he had become the strange. Wearing a kippah outside became an act of bravery.

Here, people thought their bigotry was polite. Women would approach him in the grocery store to tell him that their congregation "prayed for the Jews." They would ask him questions, try to explain Jesus to him, even laugh in his face and explain that Jesus was a Jew and so the Jews shouldn't have a problem converting. They got especially ornery when Ari explained that Jesus wasn't considered a prophet by the Jewish people. It was doubly frustrating because he was a rabbi, he was expected to always be kind, respectful. He represented the Jewish people, and he couldn't be allowed to have an off day or lose his temper lest it reflect poorly on all Jews and justify a new wave of violence against Jews.

Marginalized groups and people suffered under the weight of that responsibility every time they had an interaction with the population at large. You couldn't be black and angry without proving that black people were angry. You couldn't be Jewish and rude without people then going on to say that *Jewish people are rude.* So many people, even good people, formed their opinion of you based on how little you challenged them. As one of the thousands of "others" in the country, Ari had become an expert of not pressing against the comfort of the majority.

Ari wished it ended at the people he ran into, but even the governor and everyone on the right wing considered support of Israel to be the same thing as respecting the Jewish people. How many times had he gotten into arguments with people about politicians who kowtowed to white supremacists' dog whistles and Neo-Nazi rhetoric, only to be told that those politicians couldn't possibly be anti-Jewish because they supported Israel? How many times had people on the left explained to him that Jews were evil because of the actions the nation of Israel took regarding the Palestinians? It didn't matter to them what Ari believed or how he voted. What mattered was that he was Jewish. Therefore, in their minds, he *was* Israel, he was *all* Jews, and he bore the weight of their sins, imagined or real. It didn't matter that these thoughts and beliefs might be politically driven or that they had been in place since European kinds devised rhetoric in order to take land from Jewish citizens. People didn't care what was real, who their Jewish neighbors were, they cared about their own agenda and preconceived notions. Never mind the anti-Semitic dogma behind those notions. The dogma that was driving Aiden King to attack right now.

+

Dan joined Ari, standing beside him, supporting Father Jeremy, who had refused to sit still. The three of them squared off with King and his horrifying pet. Dan remembered Ari mentioning the gun in the office; if they could distract King long enough, maybe one of them could make a break for it, grab the firearm, and end this nightmare.

"Well, ain't that a shame, Joseph?" King sighed, clucking his tongue as though the three men were simply petulant toddlers in need of correcting. "I had hoped to come here and bring the light of Christ to a Jew, but I find that even my brothers in Christ stand in solidarity with denying Christ's love. I expected better, even from one so misguided as a priest."

"Well, we do stand united," Dan spat. "So you should just head on out." He prayed King would just turn and go, but he knew he wouldn't. The other option was to delay violence as long as possible. He had pressed his cell-phone into Muneed's hands and told her to call 911. If they could stay alive long enough, maybe the cops could get here, a whole swat team to deal with this lunatic. Then again, according to Jose before he had been beheaded, the city was already collapsing into riots.

The four men stood staring at each other, but only King had a smile on his face, only King knew how things would progress.

# Abhorrent Faith

# Chapter 3

"You keep making demands, but you are in no place to demand anything of anyone." Aiden King mocked the Methodist preacher before crossing his arms over his chest.

"So, you're just keeping us here for your own sick and sadistic amusement?" Dan demanded, nearly shouting and making Ari wince.

"I will not hesitate to unleash Joseph on those who refuse the will of God, who refuse to walk in righteousness. I speak for the Lord. I am cruel insomuch as the Lord is cruel. Call me sick if you think the Lord is sick! And I am only sadistic in his name that has come to cleanse and save us all!"

Ari tensed; he wished Dan would stop antagonizing the madman. Who knew what he would do next, or rather, what he would have the monster at his heels do?

"But you want to know the true tragedy? The awful truth? I didn't come to hurt anyone, that's not my purpose. I came here to bring the light of Jesus Christ to the Jews, to be a part of the saving of souls. You stand against me in a holy mission." He sighed dramatically, as though he were the one who was the victim of cruel injustice instead of a monster who whet his appetite on the wholesale slaughter of marginalized peoples.

The idiocy and horror of it was staggering. Throughout history, Jews had been given this choice, time after time, by group after group. The annals of history were coated in the blood of the martyrs made of Jews and rabbis who had refused to convert even in name. Martin Luther, Mohammad, countless popes, kings, emperors, and assorted scum had set the choice before the Jewish people. Sainthood and respect were given to those who held strong, ridicule and hate for those who gave in. Even one of the so-called false messiahs, Shabbatai Tzevi, had been given the choice: convert to Islam or lose your head. He had converted, earning the scorn of everyone and losing all pretense of holiness he had once held.

Part of the process of conversion asked those converting to pledge their fate to that of the Jews. Ari had made the joke once in a while, before 2016, that in 20th century America, that wasn't such a big ask. Those jokes seemed so far away now, so distant and painful. He was called on to make that pledge, to make that stand, to sacrifice not only himself but others, in the name of what? Pride? Was not the key tenant of Jewish law the preservation of life? And while one could become a martyr in protection of their faith and in deference to HaShem, was it also considered righteous to send others, goyim, to their deaths for your pride? There were lessons and mitzvot that stated that one of the things that was worth dying for was admitting to converting in front of other Jews. But he was the only Jew here at the moment. Ari thought of his wife; she was with the children and teenagers upstairs. If she came back while this killer was here, if the children saw this ... and what about when the parents came back? He needed to defuse this situation as quickly as possible.

"So ... if I convert to Christianity, you'll let us all go?" Ari asked.

Aiden King shook his head. "I'm not a moron,

rabbi. I know you'll just claim to accept Jesus into your heart and renounce him the second the sword of Judah no longer hangs over your throat. No, I want to save you, to convince you of Jesus's true power and the truth of his word. We'll have a … friendly debate."

Ari's mouth hung open in shock. A woman was dying, Jeremy was gravely injured, this man, this killer had terrorized them. And all the man wanted to do was rehash history's greatest crimes against the Jews. Throughout history, Christians in power had demanded or invited Jewish rabbis and scholars to argue and debate points of Torah and the Christian bible. They were always dressed up as cordial, friendly, and civilized. But the truth was that when the Jewish delegate didn't convert or roll over and admit that the Christian bible was the true word of God, it went to bloodshed. Sometimes of an individual, more often of an entire community. Ari was about to argue against the absurdity of the demand when Dan interrupted him.

"A debate? Against Ari? What kind of debate?" Dan asked.

Ari shot him a look of horror. Why was he humoring the man? Of course, Ari had no way of knowing that Dan's phone was in Muneed's hands. All he knew was that the longer the man was here, the more danger everyone present was in, the longer Muneed went without medical attention, the more opportunities existed for more people to get hurt.

"The only debate that matters anymore, pastor: over the scripture. We'll discuss the scriptures, the gospels, and either rabbi Ari will come to know Jesus's love or he'll make an apostate outta me." The last was said with mirth, as though such a thing could never happen, and that was probably true.

King had the sort of overabundance of zealous belief that could not be shaken no matter what; he was the sort who saw God's love in every child with cancer and Jesus's might in every natural disaster. *The child would have been gay* he would say. Or, *It's because Kanye got a divorce that Jesus sent that typhoon to Malaysia.* Of course, men like this, they never sought to find the meaning within disasters that struck their own people. When Tony Perkins's home was destroyed by a flood just weeks after he claimed that God used natural disasters to punish gay men and women, the community was silent.

When Joel Osteen's congregation was attacked because they had closed the doors to their church during the flooding, the community was silent. And when the Westboro church had taken to arms and unleashed carnage on the streets before being driven underground … where was the outrage? It was a zealotry that could pardon the worst of humanity's crimes while simultaneously demonizing natural love.

Ari's attention was less on King's words, his eyes were glued to King's mouth, on his teeth. There were too many of them; they seemed to go at odd angles and be too sharp. He looked down at Joseph, the thing King had brought with him. The man was barely recognizable as a man anymore. His skin was slimy and pale, his veins pulsing with a horrible red light just beneath the surface. All along his body, bony growths that shined with some slick mucus jutted at incongruous angles. They hadn't been there when the monster first attacked, Ari was sure. Even as he watched, he saw the creature seem to swell with new musculature. Muscles were moving and changing just beneath the nearly translucent pale skin.

What could do that to a man? What could

change him into a monster, cause him to mutate and serve another man? The only possible answer Ari could think of was a virus, but that seemed too ludicrous. That was the stuff of Hollywood films and video games. Not reality. Whatever the truth was, it looked like Aiden King was suffering from it too. Would he morph into a monster before their eyes? Would he start killing? And maybe most importantly, was that why he was able to control Joseph Moore?

Ari believed in God, but he was more of a humanist or universalist. He was a devout Jew, but he believed it was one path towards the divine and towards healing the world. He hadn't put much thought into supernatural events other than as useful lessons and mysteries to unravel within the text and fun folktales for the community. King was saying that this was supernatural, that God was doing this, or the devil; Ari always had a hard time understanding the duality of Christian theology. Even with the display of monstrosity, complete with the diabolic red glow that emanated not only from Joseph Moore but from Aiden King as well, Ari still could not believe that what was happening was some punishment from God. He simply didn't believe in that sort of vindictive, violent deity.

"Well, rabbi? Will you have a civilized theological discussion with me, examine your own shrouded misconceptions of the scripture, or will I have Joseph here finish what he began?" King let his hand fall to Joseph's shoulder. The man panted, letting out a pained whine. Strands of thick phlegmy drool dripped from his maw as he pawed at the ground with clawed fingers.

This was it; this was the moment he had to make a choice. Would he stand proud, or would he stand down? Allowing his faith and personal ideals to get others killed was not in his nature. But every moment they spent down here was another moment where Sarah or the children might come in. If Aiden King killed the four of them now, would he leave without ever knowing about and thus sparing Sarah and the children who hid upstairs?

Ari slowly nodded. He could sacrifice himself for his wife and the congregation's children, but he couldn't make that choice for Dan, Jeremy, and Muneed. He just had to pray that whatever else happened, Sarah would stay upstairs with the children until this nightmare was over.

"Okay. I'll debate with you." Ari finally gave in.

# Abhorrent Faith

# Chapter 4

Jeremy watched as Ari agreed to Aiden King's ludicrous demands. Jeremy knew who King was; at least, he thought he did. They had never actually met, but he had seen King at various protests and counterprotests over the last decade. The man was exactly the sort of person, the sort of religious extremist, that gave every Christian a bad name. He was always holding up signs that said things like 'God Hates Fags' or 'Jesus Wasn't Black.' Whatever the hot topic political issue of the day was, King was always there to exploit it into his particular brand of Christian nationalist hate. He had even had a public access show for a bit; Jeremy had watched it a handful of times, specifically after King's name had come up during a lawsuit involving Alex Jones and hate crimes. Jeremy had written King off as a reactionary hate farmer who used faith to gain power and money, milking controversy for whatever it was worth. Whatever the riots were outside, whatever was going on, Jeremy couldn't be surprised that Aiden King, this piece of shit, was taking advantage of it; he was only surprised King had the balls to actually get involved in any real way.

He reached down and touched the bone protruding from his arm. Now that it was tied off, it wasn't gushing blood anymore, and the painkillers were already taking effect—his head was beginning to swim so pleasantly. The bone nub at the end of his arm was numb, but he could feel the pressure as he prodded at the bone, absorbed for a moment in the strange feeling of tingles that traveled up his arm. His attention was wrenched back to the here and now as King spoke.

"Excellent! See, this is the best option. I don't care for violence. I know the Lord may bring his might and smite those who don't accept Jesus into their hearts, especially now in the end days, but I personally, I want to save as many sinners as I can."

*What bullshit*, Jeremy thought, Aiden claiming

he didn't care for violence. In every instance Jeremy had seen the lunatic, he was calling for violence. He wanted the government to round up the gays or arrest the Blacks or any number of shit-fucking insanity. The truth was that he didn't care for getting his own hands dirty, he wanted 'the followers of Christ' to do that. He represented everything that was wrong with religion. Jeremy knew the Catholic church had problems. Plenty of his fellow priests and clergy were angry at the more progressive stances that the Pope had taken in the last ten years. But Jeremy himself had stopped believing in the children's fairy tale of God or heaven years ago. He preached because it was his job and it was a job that allowed him to offer therapy and advice to those in need.

Better an atheist behind the pulpit who wanted to help than some true believer who would rather see the world burn to ash than accept a difference of opinions. At least, that's what Jeremy told himself to assuage the guilt he felt every Sunday when he told fairy tales he didn't believe in to a desperate mass of congregants.

"So how do you want to have this ... conversation?" Ari asked.

Jeremy's vision swam to the rabbi, the world traced in colors that swam in his head. A slow pulsing red seemed to tinge the edge of his vision. Ari was a good man. Jeremy felt a certain kindred spirit with the man; he was a realist, he knew that making the world a better place meant hard work, not just sitting around and praying that something might happen. That was important, Jeremy knew that was important, but was it more important than eating? His stomach twisted; he knew he needed to eat. His eyes went to the table, laden with food. There was danger here. Jeremy's gaze slid between the food and the other … well, it wasn't a person, the thing at King's feet. It was a competitor. It would fight for Jeremy's safety, his friends, his food source, and … and something else. Jeremy's mind was muddy, a miasma of confused thoughts, trying to remember what that last thing he needed was. Was that from the pills Dan had given him?

Jeremy remembered Dan was a warrior, soldier, he had fought, he could defend them. Jeremy stepped past the other men and approached the table, ignoring the growled warning from Joseph Moore as he sat at the table and began to eat. Not much meat, he would prefer meat. But he would make do with what was before him, gather his strength so that when the time came, he could help Dan defend their nest. No, not nest. What was wrong with his head?

+

Ari watched in surprise as the older priest walked to the table, ignoring the insane and deadly situation they were in, and began to eat. He wanted to say something, but Aiden King was already pontificating.

"Well, why don't we start this real simple; you can explain to me why you reject Jesus's love. Why would you choose the fires of hell?" King asked.

He asked the same way someone might ask why you prefer sour cream over applesauce. He didn't care that Jeremy had started eating. But then again, he seemed like the sort of man who would preach through a hurricane if he thought it might bring the fear of God to someone. Fear was the operative term. Ari was always amazed at groups that used fear to try and garner followers. Whether it was evangelicals like King or politicians who used immigrants and xenophobia to rule the minds of those who let their own ignorance and trepidation rule their entire personality. It, in turn, became their leader's entire personality. While Ari didn't know Aiden King, he had known plenty of fear-mongers like him; they thrived on it. The angrier and more frightened those around them were, the more it fed into their own fervor and zealotry.

"I don't think that's how ... I don't see any evidence in the Torah for an acceptance of the figure of Jesus as Messianic ..." Ari stumbled. He had listened to these debates before, sat and watched as some of his old teachers, both in New York and Israel, had explained the various intricacies of rebuffing Christian missionaries. He hoped he could pull those memories out now, dust them off and present something approaching a decent argument. He didn't care about winning or even defending Judaism so much as he cared about stalling Aiden King from violence. He cared about getting Muneed help.

"So, I think, maybe we should start with you supplying your ... proof that Jesus is in fact the Messiah." Ari shot a glance at Dan, hoping for encouragement or at least some sort of sign that he was going about this the right way, but Dan's eyes were locked onto Joseph Moore. Ari couldn't blame him, the thing that had, at one point just a few minutes ago, been human was now changing even as they started this pitiful charade. He pulled his attention back to King, who was watching him thoughtfully.

"All right, if that's how you want to play this, I'll go ahead and offer you some proof first." King smiled wide, too wide, and placed his bible on the table, flipping it open with one hand. His eyes, hazel and bloodshot, didn't leave Ari, his predatory gaze reminiscent of some wild beast waiting to pounce. "Let's start with the easiest, in John 1:1, *In the beginning was the word, and the word was with God and the word was God!* And then in verse 14, *The word became flesh and made his dwelling among us. We have seen his glory, the glory of the one and only son, who came from the father full of grace and truth.* Pretty firm statement of Jesus being one with God. Jesus is the word, the word is God, ergo Jesus is God. And not only this, but he is full of grace and truth, and his truth speaks that only through him is the path to heaven, there is no path forward but through him." King set his hand flat on the gold trimmed pages of his bible, smiling triumphantly.

Ari stared back at him for a moment, taken aback by the confidence the man exuded, though he shouldn't have been surprised. He looked between Dan, Jeremy, and King before shaking his head. "I'm sorry, I, I don't think I can argue against your Christian bible, every line in it is designed to show Jesus as messiah."

"Of course it is, that's the entire point of the entire bible, salvation through the grace of Jesus Christ!" King snapped, irritation that Ari was not already falling to his knees in supplication plain to read in his features.

Had the preacher really thought that a single quote from the Christian Bible tacked onto a verse from Genesis would be enough to break apart Ari's entire six-thousand-year-old faith?

"Yes, it's the entire point of the Christian bible, but you can't use the Christian bible to prove the Christian bible is true, that isn't ... well that isn't an acceptable argument. I had asked, what evidence found in Torah is there?"

King snarled, his lips pulling away from receded gums that gave way to uneven too-sharp teeth. "This is why this world is going to hell, why the anti-Christ walks among us, because you fucking heathens refuse to listen to the word of God, but you want me to use the *Old* Testament?" King stressed the word *old*, emphasizing his lack of respect for the Jewish faith and its holy texts. "What about the prophet Isaiah? Is that an acceptable source for you?"

Ari opened his mouth but paused before speaking. He wanted to avoid triggering any outbursts or violence from the preacher. Should he have just smiled and nodded and treated the man's *proof* as if it were valid? He closed his mouth and swallowed, trying to recreate some of the moisture that fear had sucked out of him. "Yes, Isaiah is a fine source," Ari finally agreed.

"Thank Jesus!" King shouted, his hand rising in the air in praise before slamming down to flip through his bible. He landed on whatever passage he was looking for and thrust his finger at the page as though he were sacrificing a lamb on the altar of the Temple of Jerusalem. "Isaiah 52:13, *Behold my servant shall deal prudently, he shall be exalted and extolled and be very high.*" King held up his other hand, offering one finger as if to say 'just wait for it.' "*As many were astonished at thee; his visage was so marred more than any man, and his form more than the sons of men.* And then just a few verses later, Isaiah says, *But he was wounded for our transgressions, he was bruised for our iniquities: the chastisement of our peace was upon him; and with his stripes we are healed. All we like sheep have gone astray; we have turned every one to his own way; and the LORD hath laid on him the iniquity of us all. He was oppressed, and he was afflicted, yet he opened not his mouth: he is brought as a lamb to the slaughter, and as a sheep before her shearers is dumb, so he openeth not his mouth."* King lifted his hand palm up towards the roof, as though overcome by the holiness of the imagery Isaiah described. "This, this you can't say isn't directly about Jesus being beaten and dying for all of our sins!"

Ari glanced at Dan, wishing that the other preacher would speak up or help the situation in any way, but Dan's eyes were on Jeremy, who was messily eating, using his one hand to shovel food into his mouth.

"Jeremy?" Dan stuttered.

Jeremy Fennec looked up from the food. His eyes were wide and frantic, they pulsed with an unsteady red glow. Whatever was happening to Joseph Moore and Aiden King was beginning to infect the priest.

Ari risked a look back at Muneed, praying she could hold on until help, the police or fire department, arrived. Even from across the room, he could see her chest rising and falling. She was alive, but her breaths seemed shuddering, like each was labored and painful. He was sure they were. But so long as she was alive, there was hope.

Ari shook his head, bringing his attention back to the threat at hand and the task that King had assigned him. "There are a few problems with that proof. The first is that you say that it obviously refers to Jesus, but I don't see that as being the case. Both of us have studied the bible through the lens of our beliefs. You've spent your life reading Isaiah with the assumption that it was directed at Jesus, while I was never taught that. I read these verses at least once a year without ever connecting the two."

"How?" howled Aiden. "How could you be so blind to read the words and not connect this to your Lord and savior? Explain that to me!"

"He's trying to!" Dan snapped, taking a step forward but stopping when he heard Joseph Moore let out a wet, gurgling growl.

"It's okay, Dan ..." Ari whispered, trying to keep everyone calm when he didn't feel calm himself. "So, it starts with *behold my servant, he shall be exalted and extolled.* Well, I've been taught this referred to the Jewish people, who are often identified in the singular as Israel. *As many were astonished at thee; his visage was so marred more than any man.* This has changed over the years, but again directly addresses the Jewish people, pogroms, expulsions, the inquisition, the holocaust. Have we not as a people borne the world's iniquities? Have we not been treated unkindly? You say this is about Jesus, but Jesus didn't bear his execution silently; he opened his mouth according to your own bible. He screamed out to God, blasphemed, asking why God had forsaken him. This can't refer to Jesus then. But there are Jewish martyrs who suffered just as much if not more than Jesus and did so without blaspheming, rebuking God."

"You're just twisting the words of the past to fit with what Jews have been through since, distorting the facts to suit your needs," King accused. "Which you have to do, and yes, terrible things have happened to you Jews, but nothing that wasn't earned! Why have there been pogroms? Why have you been kicked out of every country your kind makes home? Why did the holocaust happen? Because it's punishment, a curse earned from God when you scum murdered Jesus, when you killed

God's own flesh and blood!"

The scathing accusation hung in the air. Ari didn't bat an eye at that one, but he could see how agitated Dan looked. He worried that the minister may not be able to hold his tongue for much longer.

"Just twisting words? I, well, look at Matthew." He gestured at King's bible on the table. "In Matthew, the author—"

"Matthew was the author, in case that was too hard for you to follow," King said, a sardonic chuckle shaking his weak jowls.

"The author," Ari continued, "describes Pontius Pilate as a kind, gentle man, who strives for peace and to protect the innocent. In Matthew, Pontius attempts to spare Jesus over and over again."

"And the Jews insist on his murder, insist that Jesus dies despite his innocence and grace!" King agreed.

"Okay, but that's not what happened, or at least that is completely incongruous with actual history."

"So, you were there, you saw all this happen? Because Matthew *was* there. And did see it happen."

"No, but every historian's account and every bit of evidence we have about the time period makes that account completely unbelievable. Philo, a respected historical source, stated that Pontius was a cruel, reckless man who was prone not only to corruptibility but also to torture, violence, robbing citizens, and mass executions! He was such a wicked man that even Rome couldn't stomach his crimes and recalled him to be sanctioned. Does that sound like the sort of man who would strive to protect an innocent man? And if the account of Pontius Pilate is completely off base, then what else has been twisted in order to tell a story that the author wanted?" Ari was aware he was stressing the concept that the book was not written by a Jewish man named Matthew but rather some other figure, most likely Saul of Tarsis. He could see that King was irritated, agitated, ready to blow a gasket.

"You have to look at all the examples, not just the ones that suit your explanation, of Isaiah 52, for instance, many would point at rabbi Akiva, who was a great man, and many considered him a miracle worker. He violated the Roman statute forbidding the teaching of Torah in about 100 C.E. and because of that, was flayed alive by Turnus Rufus. Despite that, during his horrifying execution, Akiva sang the Sh'ma, praising God.

I feel like that is more in line with this prophecy than Jesus."

Ari could tell by the look on King's face that mentioning Akiva had been a mistake.

# Abhorrent Faith

# Chapter 5

"I've never heard of this Akiva," King spat.

"Well, I'm not particularly surprised. How many famous rabbis do you know?" Ari asked, trying to quickly salvage his side of the conversation. "There have been miracle workers like the Baal Shem Tov and the Maharal, Maimonides, the Rambam, and many others, even a few who have claimed to be the messiah. There are, to this day, people who venerate the Lubavitcher rabbi and believe he is not dead."

"They didn't spread. Do you understand why they didn't spread? They didn't spread because they didn't have the power of God behind them the way Jesus does. Christianity has spread throughout the world, and every knee will bend to his throne; that should be enough proof that Jesus is King."

"Well, if you want to talk about followers ..." Dan cut in. "What about Islam or Buddhism? If we're talking sheer number of followers."

"They don't come close to the number of Christians in the world!" King snarled.

"Are you sure about that?" Dan asked. He was sure the sheer size of the population of places like India and China would make that stat impossible, but Ari was nodding.

"That's true, actually, but it doesn't mean anything, first because the size of a group has never meant that group is particularly correct about anything, and also Jeremiah the prophet said that *and they shall no more teach every man his neighbor, saying know HaShem, for they shall all know me.*"

"You're quoting my arguments now? And the word you said instead of Lord, I don't want you twisting scripture," King warned.

"HaShem, it means the name, it's another name for God, that's all. As for your arguments, Jeremiah says that you won't need to tell or teach or proselytize any longer, for everyone will accept God. The very fact that we can talk about which religion is the largest means that not every heart knows HaShem, therefore, Jesus couldn't have been the messiah, he hasn't fulfilled that prophecy."

"That's because that prophecy is dealing with the second coming of Jesus."

"Okay, let's say that's true. Then why do Christians claim to have a new covenant and not need to follow any of the Mitzvot that are commanded in Torah?"

"Because in the same scripture you're quoting, just as Satan himself can ..." King spent a few seconds flipping back to Jeremiah in his bible, scanning the verses to find what he was looking for. "Jeremiah says *I took them by the hand to bring them out of Egypt, which my covenant they broke, but this shall be the covenant that I will make with the house of Israel, after those days, saith the Lord, I will put my law in their inward parts!* This clearly means that there is a new covenant to be made, one created by Jesus and humanity. "

"So, when God took the Jews out of Egypt, which it mentions there, and gave them Torah, that isn't the covenant mentioned?" Ari asked. King's mouth moved up and down, but Ari continued. "And if we accept that verses 31 through 33 are in reference to the lifetime of Jesus in 29 C.E., you're saying that one verse down, with no context, subtext, or change in phrase, they skip more than two thousand years ahead? That just doesn't make sense."

"Well, I'm sorry that prophecy is so hard for you to grasp!" King stuttered, his voice growing more and more phlegmatic.

Dan watched the verbal jousting; his head was swimming slightly. It could be the hydrocodone he had taken right before the attack, or it could be the situation they found themselves in. On one hand, King was everything Dan hated about faith and religion; he was a killer who had brought terror and panic to him and his friends. On the other ... on the other, his friend was directly attacking his beliefs, the core of who he had been his entire life, reinterpreting scripture and verses Dan had held close to his heart in a way that made him feel ridiculous and stupid. It set his teeth on edge. He wanted to shout, to be involved, but he felt powerless.

"Listen," Ari offered, "the problem with prophecy, if we assume it is real, if we assume that everything in Torah is to be taken literally and out of its historic context, which I don't think anyone who looks at it logically can do—"

"It is the word of God most high and MUST be taken literally," King snarled. His moods swung from moment to moment, sometimes triumphant and smug and seconds later, psychotic and dangerous. He raised a shaky hand to point at the rabbi; the fingers spasmed and twitched as though every muscle was fighting against him. "You'll argue against the very word of God if it means you can deny your true Lord!"

Ari rubbed the bridge of his nose, clearly frustrated by the surreal nightmare he found himself in.

Dan could sympathize, his body didn't have any more adrenaline to keep him going; he could feel exhaustion pulling at him. Hunger too, he was envious of Jeremy getting to sit and eat. But as hungry as he was, and as annoying as Ari's arguments were, he couldn't abandon him.

Ari probably didn't want to pick even more of a fight with this madman, but he also couldn't see a way out. Perhaps like Dan, Ari was too exhausted mentally to continue biting his tongue.

"The word of God? Are you saying every word of your King James bible is the literal word of

God?"

"Yes, that is exactly what I'm saying," King snapped.

Joseph rose from his haunches, obviously agitated by King's irritation.

"Okay, but let's look at that. According to Jewish tradition, the Hebrew bible is made up of the Torah, which God handed to Moses at Sinai, right? The literal word of God. Then we have Kings and Writings, which include prophecy. Kings was written by Hebrew kings like Solomon and David; they weren't God, they were men, deeply flawed men at that. And as for the prophets, I suppose you could also make the argument for their writings being the word of God, though again, it would be filtered through the minds and hearts of flesh and blood men. Then we get to the Christian bible—"

"The New Testament," King corrected.

"We avoid terms like that because it implies that the Torah is old or outdated." In times of stress, the muscle memory motor functions of teaching returned to Ari.

Dan almost smiled at the near autonomic nature of Ari's desire to teach.

"It *is* outdated, that's the fucking point." King

sneered.

Jeremy snarled something that didn't seem recognizable as words. His face was pale and clammy, his mouth looked wider, and his hands twitched, bulging as if budding new growth was trying to burst through his skin.

"And look at that," King continued. "Your priest is marked by the beast. Soon, he will join the army of righteousness under my control as we spread the word of Jesus Christ ... once I am done here."

Jeremy huffed. His eyes seemed to expand in his skull, the sockets moving like putty as his oversized eyes bulged. Bits of pasta salad dripped between teeth that sat uneven in the priest's mouth. He was barely recognizable as the man he had once been.

Dan couldn't begin to imagine what the priest was feeling, thinking. Was the man he had been still there? Would he really be under the control of King? What the hell was going on?

"Whatever you want to call it," Ari said, "it's made up of the gospels according to Matthew, Mark, Luke, John, letters from people named John, and Luke, James, and Peter, and of course, most everything could be called *letters from Paul*. A Roman Jew who had clear reason to glorify the

Roman gentiles and demonize the trouble-making Jews at the time. None of those people are God, even if you accept as a given that Jesus *is* God, which I don't, the only parts of the Christian bible capable of being called the word of God is the places in which Jesus is directly quoted. The rest is human. And humans are flawed."

"Is that your argument? That the apostles weren't God? They spoke for and spread the word of God, that is precisely who they were, their words are God's words. I don't know if you're a rabbi or Satan himself!" King argued.

Ari shook his head and took a step back. He wanted to pace, he wanted to have room to think, but he knew that if he moved too much, too quickly, King would sic the abomination that was Joseph Moore on him. "I'm just a rabbi, which means I spent a lot of time in school studying religious texts, not just the Torah but hundreds of texts, like the Talmud. And I've read the King James Bible." Ari frowned as King shook his head. "I have *read* it. Christians seem to think that when someone doesn't believe in Jesus, they're either a Satanist or ignorant. I'm neither."

"What you don't understand, because you

deny the existence of the devil, is that you *are* his servant. The greatest lie the devil ever told was to convince the world he didn't exist! And yet for any true Christian, we see his influence everywhere. In the homosexuals invading cities, in the heathen terrorists being ushered in by diabolic politicians who kowtow to the Satanic socialist propaganda! Satan can be seen in every single child afflicted with autism or calling themselves trans, when all they do is spit in the face of god and say *Satan, I am with you!*"

Dan couldn't hold his tongue anymore. "That's bullshit. We aren't your Sunday evening church crowd, we aren't sycophantic old ladies who you scare into sending you a few thousand dollars out of our social security, you fucking parasite." His anger was getting the better of him, controlling him, he wanted to tear Aiden King apart with his teeth and claws, no …. hands … he didn't have claws. "Autism isn't evil or a death sentence or hurting anyone, those are good and innocent children. Trans kids are children, children trying to fit in. People who, no fuck you, children who are among the highest for suicide risk because fucks like you want to get in and call them evil."

"By rejecting their own flesh, they reject God's perfection, they are harbingers of the devil! And everyone who speaks softly to avoid upsetting the PC culture that Satan has wrapped around these mongrel faggots who can't be grateful for God's love deserve the coward's death they give themselves!"

Dan roared. He had two trans kids in his church's youth group; their struggles were what had initially brought him to the interfaith community. He took three steps forward towards King. By the time he saw Joseph Moore rising from the floor to intercept him, he knew he had fucked up and that he would be killed. Dan jerked to a stop, trying to reverse his momentum. Terror at the sight of the oncoming Moore filled him, and he only managed to fall backwards on his ass. But before Moore reached him, another form slammed into the killer, flinging him to the side.

Jeremy stood there, his shirt ripped in several places, torn by new muscles bulging through the fabric. His jaw hung loose as massive tusks grew from the lower mandible. He let out a discordant scream and charged Moore again. The severed arm had swelled, rending the tourniquet, but it wasn't bleeding. Now, long fleshy growths like boneless whips of skin and knotted horn grew where his arm had been.

Dan watched in amazement as the two monsters rolled across the floor of the auditorium. Neither of them could be said to be human any longer; but if they weren't human, then what were they? Dan had to admit they looked like demons. The glow of red that pulsed from their veins and eyes, the misshapen bone poking through the skin like horns and claws, the slavering rage and hunger with which they now howled at each other—it was all demonic. But they didn't smell demonic. The scent they carried was natural, normal, easy to accept. But at the same time, it was jarring. Four males in one place vying for food and, more importantly, a female; that was dangerous.

Dan grunted, squeezing his eyes tight together and dispelling those thoughts. He didn't have any desire to fight for food or the injured Muneed. And they didn't smell fine. He hadn't noticed before with all the chaos, but Moore reeked. It was a sick, sour scent that reminded Dan of infection, something he had seen plenty of during his time in the service. He opened his eyes again as the growling from the two former-men grew to a crescendo.

Jeremy was on top of Moore, his tusks drilling into the other man's chest, gouging out chunks of knotted muscle and flesh. For his part, Moore was struggling to get off his back, his grotesquely swollen hands pounding into Jeremy's sides and back. His claws left long gashes that oozed glowing blood. The smell of musk thickened in the air, pungent and nauseating. But still, Dan found that the display of rending flesh and the thick smell of male wasn't upsetting, it was invigorating; he had half a mind to go over there and help Jeremy deal with the rival. His stomach twisted painfully, and he forced his mind back to reason.

Jeremy's whip-like appendage came up, and the priest lashed down, striking with the appendage like a scorpion's tail. Each rise and fall brought a howl of pain and rage from Moore as he was punctured and sliced. It seemed a forgone conclusion that Jeremy would win this fight, but what then? Would he be under King's control the way Moore was? Dan risked a glance at King; the preacher was shouting but couldn't be heard over the roars and barks of the two monsters. He was red in the face, his horrible eyes stretched wide as he shouted and waved his hand in the air. Probably rebuking Jeremy in the name of racist Jesus.

Moore, it turned out, wasn't done. He opened his mouth, and a thick gangrenous tongue lashed out, slapping against Jeremy's malformed face. Where it hit, the skin hung in tatters. The organ had sprouted serrated teeth that dug into Jeremy and pulled the flesh apart. The tongue lashed out again and again, ripping bits of Jeremy's lips and nose off and dragging them into Moore's maw to be devoured. Another lash dug into Jeremy's eye, popping the swollen orb like a water balloon filled with pus. It splattered Moore's face and oozed down Jeremy's eye socket. But Moore ignored both, instead digging his fibrous muscular tongue into Jeremy's skull. The sound of Jeremy's flesh and brain being torn into by the toothsome tongue made Dan's stomach roll; but whether it was with horror or hunger, he didn't know.

Moore pushed the flailing and panicking Jeremy off of him and rose, screaming in triumph as he dug in Jeremy's skull. His celebration was short lived as Jeremy reached up with a single claw and severed Moore's tongue. Dan's heart swelled with hope but quickly sank again. Jeremy was staggering, his frantic swipes at Moore were getting weaker, more haphazard. He was slowing down. Moore knew it too. He stalked around Jeremy in a tight circle before pouncing on Jeremy's back and tearing into the flesh there. His teeth, oddly angled and crooked, nevertheless found purchase and tore through flesh, muscle, and bone. The sound of Jeremy's spine crunching between Moore's teeth echoed in the auditorium space, followed by the nauseating sound of Moore lapping up the fluid that leaked out.

Dan licked his lips. His stomach was emptiness incarnate, a bottomless void that dragged his willpower and everything that he was down into it. That was his friend being killed, but all Dan could do was grapple with the crisis of faith and hunger in his own mind. What if King was right? What if this was the mark of the beast and all of his backwoods southern relatives who railed against the LGBT community and abortion were right? He couldn't believe that. He believed in a loving god, a kind god. A god that loved humanity so much that he sent his only son to die in order to save everyone.

He glared at Ari from the corner of his eye. His so-called friend was trying dismantle his faith. While King might be a monster, at least he was a monster that accepted Jesus ... No, no, Ari wasn't his enemy. Dan didn't subscribe to this us-versus-them mentality. And these weren't demons. They couldn't be demons. It had to be something else, mass hysteria, drugs. Drugs made sense, he had done plenty of drugs in his life. This was a bad trip, a shared hallucination, or maybe it was just a nightmare. Please, God, let it be a nightmare.

Whatever had happened to Moore had happened to Jeremy after the attack. Dan looked over at Muneed, the female. Would she turn into a monster too? He didn't know. He needed to know, he needed to know that she was okay. With Jeremy dead, there was one less rival to worry about. He ran to check on her, ignoring Ari's protests.

+

Ari stood alone against King now. Moore was busy eating Jeremy's still twitching corpse in a display that turned his stomach, and Dan had run off without a word to check on Muneed. Ari looked up at King, who was staring intently with his wide, psychotic eyes. His lips were peeled back from his teeth in what Ari assumed was a smile, but there was no warmth or joy in the smile. It was the sort of smile that men wore when they knew they would win and get their way. The sort of smile that men wore when they were going to teach their wives not to be late with dinner. The sort of smile men wore when they were going to teach their sons not to fail tests. It was the expression of a man who was used to having power and never tired of using it.

Ari had seen the face often enough on politicians, on husbands who thought they were going to get away with abuse, on the worst that humanity had to offer. King was no exception.

"Look, four people are dead. Can we stop this? We can still get Muneed medical attention, we can still—" Ari paused, trying not to gag as the sound of gristle popping between Moore's teeth as he ripped Jeremy's face off to chew reached him. He didn't proselytize because he didn't feel the need to. He didn't care what Christians believed so long as they kept it to their own faith and stopped trying to drag Jews into it with them. "Please ..."

King's smile stretched unnaturally wide, his thin, cruel lips parting in a rasping breath as he seemed to drink in the moment of the Jewish man pleading with him. "Psalm 22, from King David," the pastor stated.

# Abhorrent Faith

# Chapter 6

Ari groaned. He didn't want to debate, he hadn't wanted to when it began, and now another one of his friends, another good man, lay dead with a monster defiling his corpse not ten feet away. He had no stomach for it.

King, however, seemed to sense Ari's weakness and pressed on. *"My God, my God, why have you forsaken me, why are you so far from helping me and from the words of my roaring? Our fathers trusted in You, they trusted and were delivered ... But I am a worm, and no man; a reproach of men, and despised of the people. All they that see me laugh me to scorn. Thou art God from my mother's belly ... I am poured out like water, and all my bones are out of joint."* King paused, trembling, his ugly mouth stretched in an O as if he were experiencing orgasmic euphoria. His breath came in shallow gasps. It was obscene, and Ari felt like he should look away for a moment. *"For dogs have compassed me; the assembly of wicked have enclosed me; they pierced my hands and my feet ... they part my garments among them and cast lots upon my vesture."*

King lowered his arms. Ari was beginning to see the pattern; he imagined King always did this, no matter what sermon he was giving. Read every line of text trembling as if he were in sexual ecstasy to prove to his congregation that he was so faithful that God gave him pleasure. It was the kind of reading one would expect from someone who had read but never studied the text. That was the whole problem. If King wanted to believe every word of the Christian bible, more power to him. The problem was that he not only twisted the Hebrew bible to suite him but used the Hebrew bible to demonize the downtrodden and fleece honest people out of their savings. That and the murder. The murder and monsters were also problems. But while watching Dan check on Muneed, he had seen the cell phone near them. Someone could call the police, the ER, Dan could get help, he just needed time.

Ari exhaled, silently sending of a prayer of thanks to God for giving Dan a steady head on his shoulders. He understood finally why Dan encouraged this: it was stalling. "Psalm 22, written by King David, you jumped around the verse, and I can see why you're excited, but there are some problems with using Psalm 22 to justify Jesus as the messiah." He raised a hand to stave off King's objections. "First, David isn't a prophet. He was a king and a writer of beautiful, divinely inspired poetry, but not a prophet. Second, you mistranslated the verse. It isn't *pierced my hands and feet*. The word you're translating to mean pierced is actually koari, which means like a lion."

Ari had to admit the look of confusion that replaced the smug smirk on King's face tasted sweet. "So," he continued, "it would be better translated as *for dogs have surrounded me, the assembly of the wicked have enclosed me, like a lion who has my hands and my feet.* Which obviously doesn't point directly to the assumed crucifixion. There's also the issue that this was written centuries before the mythology of Jesus was written down."

"Mythology!" King gasped, clearly gearing up to go into a fire and brimstone rant.

"The gospels, then, centuries before the gospels were written," Ari relented. "Meaning the gospels could be written in such a way as to conform to what was expected from the Tanakh."

"The fuck is the Tanakh?" King sneered.

"The Hebrew bible. The Torah is just the first five books, the rest ..." Ari trailed off at the blank expression written across King's wide, freakish eyes. They were watery blue, bloodshot, and terrifying, like the big flat eyes of some demonic fish. King was one of those who believed that the Bible was one book, one text, and that any other text or studies were useless. They were people who would look at the Talmud and scoff at the idea of studying how other people interpreted sacred texts. It was an alien concept to Ari, whose entire life had been surrounded by books about books. The entirety of his religious upbringing had been centered around the concept of always asking questions and welcoming debate. Aiden King was a man to whom religious debate meant that he screamed and brought his brand of brimstone and hellfire down on someone until they were so browbeaten that they didn't have the energy to argue anymore.

King paced a little, moving slowly around near the doors. Was he agitated? Did he want to end this? If he was having second thoughts and left without hurting anyone else, that would be enough. *Please, God*, Ari thought, *please let him just leave*. But if God was listening to Ari, then King's armor of bigotry and hate was impenetrable even to the word of the sovereign of the universe. King took several steps towards Ari, who tensed in nervous anticipation, before he let out a laughing bark and then turned back towards Moore to rejoin the monster.

"This is why no one can stand Jews. Every time I give you a good argument for Jesus, you move the damn goalposts. I can't use the gospels, the testament of Jesus Christ; I can't use the writings of King David or King Solomon, the wisest man to ever live!"

Ari had to resist the urge to roll his eyes. This was the problem with zealots like Aiden King and so many others, those who felt the bible was the literal word of God refused to listen to historians. They considered the bible a historical, legal, and scientific document. Ari considered the Torah to be sacred literature but didn't consider sacred to mean unquestionable.

"Prophets and just the first five books is all you want to acknowledge." King sighed, shaking his head as though disappointed.

"We consider not just the Torah and prophets but also the writings of things, the Mishnah, the Talmud, the Zohar, countless books and arguments and treatises. But if you want us to abandon our faith and join yours, you need a very ironclad argument for the truth of Jesus. Even the concept of the messiah as you present it is—" Ari paused, trying to find the right words. "It isn't in line with what we expect, it isn't what we expect it to be. We don't expect the messiah to die for our sins, we don't feel the need for that sort of savior."

"You know, no matter what I say, you'll argue about why it isn't relevant. It's exhausting," King said with no self-awareness or sense of irony. "Isaiah, 64, *But we are all as an unclean thing, and all our righteousnesses are as filthy rags, and we all do fade as the leaf, and our iniquities, like the wind have taken us away.* Now combine that with Ecclesiastes 7:20, *For there is not a just man upon earth that does good and sinneth not.* It proves the need for something that will wash away the sins of all men, a messiah who saves not our physical bodies but our immortal souls! And then you go back to Leviticus. *And whatsoever man there be of the house of Israel, or of the strangers that sojourn among you, that shall eat any manner of blood, I will set my face against that soul that eats blood and will cut him off from among his people, For the life of the flesh is in the blood, and I have given it to you upon the altar to make an atonement for your souls: for it is the blood that maketh an atonement for the soul."*

Ari thought of Dan and Jeremy and all of the good Christians he had met over the years. He felt a twinge of guilt; he didn't want to dismantle anyone else's faith and comfort, he only wanted to stop the man from attacking his.

"Okay, that sounds convincing, and I see why you connect that to your concepts of a messiah," Ari offered tentatively. Maybe he should just give in here, he could claim that this passage convinced him. End it all here, maybe King would leave without hurting anyone else. But Ari could still hear the labored breathing from Muneed, he could hear the ripping sound as Joseph Moore ripped into Jeremy's corpse. Ari also remembered that for countless years, the church, the inquisition, and puritans would force a victim to convert before burning them at the stake. Forcing them to convert to save their souls, burning them alive to not break the rules against bloodshed. King wouldn't let any of them live, he was just trying to convert them to serve his own sick ego.

Ari pressed his lips into a thin line. "But the fact is that there are problems with this proof as well. If you read all of Isaiah, you'll see that he is speaking not about the nature of mankind but the behavior of mankind in that specific time. Claiming that we are somehow cursed and condemned to being unclean things is counter to the teachings of Torah. For instance, if we look at Deuteronomy 28, *if you shall hearken diligently unto the voice of Adonai, to observe and to do all of their mitzvot which I commanded thee"*

"Mitzvot are good deeds!" King interjected, his eyes brightening for a moment with recognition.

Ari paused, staring at the man, worried about his erratic behavior.

"Technically, it means commandments or rules. But it goes on to say, *this day, then Adonai will set thee on high above all nations, and blessed shall you be in the city and blessed shall you be in the field and blessed shall be the fruit of your body and blessed shall you be when*

94

*you come in and when you go out.* And then in verse 30, *If you hearken unto the voice of Adonai, to keep their commandments and their statutes which are written in the book of the Law,* or the Torah, *and if thou turn unto Adonai with all thine heart, and with all thine soul. For this commandment which I command thee this day, it is not hidden from thee, nor is it far off. It is not in heaven that thou should say, who shall go up for us to heaven and bring it unto us, that we may hear it. But the word is very nigh unto thee, in thy mouth, and in thy heart and thou may do it."* Ari shrugged as he finished the verse.

"This very, very clearly states that through following the mitzvot set forth in the Torah, the laws and commandments, especially the ten commandments from the tablets given to Moses, one can find their way to heaven and have heaven in their heart without any need for intermediary."

"But it isn't just the ten commandments, is it? It's six hundred and thirty commandments, near a thousand laws you have to keep every single damn day, and no man can stick with that, no man can live without sin, no man other than Jesus is perfect."

"There are certainly Chasidim that strive to

follow all relevant mitzvot," Ari returned. "A lot of those laws only apply when living in Israel or while the temple stands, so the number is substantially lower for those of us who live abroad."

"Excuses! Think then, if you have to sacrifice blood to atone for your soul as Leviticus says, and you have to do it at the temple, how can you atone now? Simple, Jesus died for it, the blood of Christ, or God himself, poured out over the world to offer atonement. In fact, since the Temple fell, there is no way *to* atone but through the blood of Christ! That's why Jesus said, 'there is no way to the father but through me!'"

"Okay, but Jesus died while the second Temple was still standing. Was it a preemptive death? Was he killed so that times of atonement could overlap? And also, the rules for blood sacrifice were strict, they included things like when the animal could be sacrificed, what you did with the blood and the meat, where the animal had to be sacrificed, and of course, maybe most importantly, it could never be a human. A living person! The sacrifice of human life is strictly forbidden in every text. Other groups and tribes engaged in human sacrifice, but the Torah, the law, forbids it. And even if we ignore all of that, Jesus wasn't sacrificed during a ritual, on an altar, at the temple. He was executed by Romans in Golgotha. His death followed none of the criteria for a purifying sacrifice."

"I'm sorry." King growled.

# Abhorrent Faith

# Chapter 7

King's knuckles were white as he gripped the edge of the little potluck table—which was a mess, Jeremy had scattered plates in his frantic urge to devour as much as possible. "You act as though the idea that there would be a messiah is foreign, but earlier you even admitted there was an expectation, there is the belief that the messiah will come! You just ignore the signs. You want to speak about what is and isn't the word of God. Well, in Deuteronomy, one of the books given to you people by God himself, verse 18, *I will raise up a prophet from among their brethren, like unto thee, and will put my words in his mouth!*"

"Yes, there are prophecies and an expectation of a messianic figure and age, but that verse is talking about prophets, not messiah. That was simply saying that there will be prophets after Moses, such as Jeremiah, Isaiah. Point in fact, just a few lines down, it says *But the prophet which shall presume to speak a word in my name, which I have not commanded him to speak ... even that prophet shall die.* Which directly speaks against false prophets, which we would consider Jesus to be."

King bellowed in response, an unearthly howl of rage that caused Moore to look up from his meal. "You would call your Lord and savior, the lamb of God, the one who died for your sins a false prophet? You would spit in his face! You dare?" Spittle flew from the man's mouth, thick and phlegmy. "You think you can ignore what parts of the bible you want to, just pretend that they aren't there. But I am here to shove them down your damned throat. In Isaiah 7—"

"I know what you're trying to say," Ari nearly shouted over King, the thought that Dan would have called the police bolstering his courage. "You think you can use the prophecy of Ahaz's savior, Immanuel, a man who lived five hundred years before Jesus to justify your beliefs?"

"It speaks plainly that the savior will come from the house of David, and we have the proof that

Joseph was descended from David!" King growled back, his teeth clenching hard enough to crack.

"Who is we? What is proof? Your proof comes from the book you're trying to prove as valid, and that isn't proof at all! And furthermore," Ari felt all his anger from years of listening to overbearing proselytizers bubbling over, his own frustration and feelings of hopelessness rising to a pitch, "who cares where Joseph was descended from? Joseph wasn't Jesus's father! According to your own gospels, Joseph assumed Mary cheated on him, he never had sex with her. Even if he had, Jewish lineage is traced through the mother! So again, this proof proves nothing!"

King pushed his chest out, his back straight; he looked like a twisted man, his veins, pulsing with red light, wriggled under his skin. His eyes, watery and bloodshot, oozed a milky white fluid as he trembled in rage. "You think you can just speak of Jesus so flippantly? I tried to save your soul, Jew. I tried to save you. But you won't be saved, you are too blinded by evil to see that Jesus is nigh, the beast walks the earth." As if on cue, the ground trembled as though a giant had taken a footstep just outside. Aiden King looked up, his eyes unfocused, seeming to look through the walls and ceiling towards the beast he claimed was outside. He raised a hand, possibly in prayer, possibly in some sort of salute. *"Do not think that I came to bring peace on earth. I did not come to bring peace but a sword. For I have come to set a man against his father. He who loves his father or mother more than me is not worthy of me, and he who loves son or daughter more than me is not worthy of me. But he who endures to the end shall be saved."*

King lowered his hand. He looked thoughtful for a moment, he looked almost like he would second guess himself, but after only a few seconds, the look of self-reflection was gone and all the hate and self-righteousness was back.

"Kill him," King hissed through clenched teeth.

Moore rose from the floor, growling. Tendons ripped from Jeremy dangled from between the offset bone tusks that filled Moore's mouth, hunger and rage bleeding in a dull red glow from his eyes.

+

Dan knelt next to Muneed. Much as he feared, the subtle red glow pulsed under the bandages he had wrapped around her waist. She was breathing, her chest rising and falling in slow intervals. Dan licked his lips, he needed to check her wound. No he didn't! If he moved the wrap that bound her wound, it could rip open any clotting that had happened. Her guts could spill back out. But on the other hand, if he did check, maybe he could make it better, maybe he could get a look at her abdomen and the smooth dark skin there.

Dan shook his head. What the fuck was that?

He didn't want to see Muneed's body. His eyes darted to the rise and fall of her chest. Did he? She was a pretty woman, but Dan had never looked at her that way before. He had never seen Muneed and thought about what it would be like to touch her, to lick her skin, to flick her nipples with his tongue while he grabbed great handfuls of her firm ass and dragged her down onto his …

Dan closed his eyes and tried desperately to dismiss the raging erection that was throbbing in his pants. This woman, Muneed, was his friend, and she was badly hurt. Why was her body the only thing he could think about? He pushed his cock down with one hand while reaching out with the other to touch her forehead. As his fingers brushed her head, her eyes shot open and she grabbed his wrist in a steel grip. She breathed heavier, panting, her eyes half lidded, dark, sexy.

"Hey ... how are you holding up?" he asked, his voice soft to avoid drawing attention from King and Moore. He could hear them behind him, but he was having trouble focusing on anything other than Muneed's eyes.

"I can smell it." She panted, her words breathy as she opened her mouth wide and licked out with a forked tongue that seemed to split as it moved to moisten her full lips.

Dan stared at the tongue. It wasn't natural, it wasn't normal. Her tongue shouldn't be like that. He knew somewhere in his brain that Muneed was being affected by the same thing that had taken Jeremy and was changing Moore and King. But try as he might, he could only think about what it would feel like to have those twin writhing tongues pressing against his cock. He swallowed, trying to control himself. He still needed food, but there was something else he needed, and a voice screaming from deep within his primal mind was commanding him that it was Muneed.

"Smell what?" he finally managed to croak out.

She rolled onto her side, and he nearly cried out but realized she didn't show any signs of being in pain. "I can smell your cum," she whispered. Her free hand, the one not clenching his wrist, landed on the painful tent of denim he had pitched in his jeans. She squeezed him through the rough fabric. "I can smell it, you want me to suck your cock, don't you?" She moaned the question, as if the very thought of having him in her mouth, her two tongues wrapped around him, milking him, was a vibrator shoved deep inside her. She released his wrist to fondle one of her breasts over her shirt.

He noticed the bony growths along her forearm and wrist, the spines that were poking from under the skin of her hand. He didn't care. He just didn't want her to stop.

Somewhere far away, a distant voice in his mind was screaming at him to stop, to help Ari. But a biological need roared in his skull, and he chewed his lip, drawing blood as his sharpening teeth tore through his flesh. He didn't care, though; he had more important things to worry about, to address. He stared down at the female frantically stroking his cock and rubbing herself. Muneed was usually so reserved, a modest and kind woman, a level headed and loving leader in the Muslim community of San Antonio. Now she was running segmented hands down her body, struggling to rip her bra off, begging him in frantic whimpers to fuck her.

He didn't want to say no, he didn't know if he would even be capable of saying no. She finally ripped off the confining material of her bra and let her breasts free. They looked swollen, plump, and heavy, perfect for feeding their young. She was the perfect mate, the perfect receptacle for his seed. He would be an idiot to allow Moore the chance to empty his balls in her instead of himself. He growled a little, surprised by the wet sound that emerged from his mouth as he reached for his belt. He swatted Muneed's hands away from his cock just long enough to rip through the leather belt and flimsy pre-cum-drenched denim that was holding his raging meat in. Muneed let out a whimper of want at the sight of his dick standing at attention for her. Her desire for him drove him on.

She grabbed his cock, and he noticed in the back of his mind that it had grown hard ridges, twisting like a corkscrew. It seeped lubricating fluid from several small spouts along the ridge. Did it always look like that? He peered at his dick for a moment, admiring his own body, from the way his stomach flexed with bulging muscles and hardened plates of armor to the design of his cock; it would penetrate deeply, it would fill Muneed and scrape any competitor's leaving clean on exit. His self-assessment of his own worthiness for fucking Muneed silly was interrupted when her clawed hand squeezed him hard. His cock squirmed in her hand, turning purple in the tight grip.

He looked up from her hand to her face. Two of her eyes, the two he had always thought were dark and beautiful, stared at him, heavy lidded, full of suggestion and need. The other 3 that pockmarked her face like ruptured boils were milky and rolled wildly. They didn't bother him or detract from her beauty.

Muneed rolled onto her stomach and pushed herself onto her knees, bracing with one clawed hand. Her other hand maintained her grip on his penis as she tugged, pulling him forward and on top of her, guiding his spiraling cock towards her pussy. He stared at her gaping sex, watching as she surrendered her hold to the writhing tendrils that sprouted from her labia to circle his dick and pull him in. Dan put two hands on her waist, pulling her against him. Despite the offering and lubrication, she was tight around his meat. With a painfully pleasureful pop that pulled a gasp from Muneed and a groan from Dan, he pushed deep into her. Inside her was heaven. His third hand, tipping the arm that sprouted from his shoulder and sported three elbows, reached forward and grabbed her hair, pulling her head back as he fucked her roughly, driven to harder heights by her encouraging moans and shouts. Thoughts of her two tongues faded from his skull as her multiple pussy feelers writhed against him, squeezing and massaging his length as he penetrated her.

He rocked his hips back and forth, loving the way her ass bounced against his pelvis with each thrust, the way her bulging back muscles shifted and moved under her skin, the light and shadow play as the bone spines that sprouted along her back tensed and relaxed with each and every movement of their bodies together.

+

Ari fell back as Moore leapt at him, scrambling back as fast as his hands and feet would allow him to. The slavering maw of the degenerate and regressed monster snapped inches from his face, and the foul reek of blood and halitosis hit Ari full in the face. He gagged, a scream on his lips. But Moore froze, his mad bloodshot eyes swiveling all around before locking back on where Dan had run to. Ari followed the gaze and nearly screamed again. Where he had expected to see the kind Methodist preacher tending to the fallen woman, he saw the two had risen and begun having sex, bestial, screaming sex. Dan pounded into Muneed from behind, his arms—too many arms—moving over her body, gripping her dark hips, and moving from her breasts to her face as though he wanted to touch all of her at once. Muneed seemed to be loving every second of it, sucking his clawed fingers into her mouth and lapping at his flesh with multiple tongues.

Ari whimpered, the sight of what his friends had become and what they were doing too much for him to take. He pushed back, away from Moore, painfully aware of the danger he was in. He was the only person in the room who wasn't exhibiting mutation and erratic behavior. But Moore seemed to have forgotten him at the sight of the two religious leaders fucking each other's brains out only a few meters away from them.

Moore rose up and bellowed a challenge with

a scream that shook the room. Dan and Muneed paused, their eyes—so many terrible bloodshot eyes—turned to this new threat. Dan pulled back, but Muneed snapped at him, reaching back and clamping his butt to keep him inside her. She rose up, grinding her hips against Dan, her breasts bouncing with every movement as she spread her clawed hands wide and roared a challenge back at Moore.

+

Dan had been ready to disentangle from his mate to defend them and kill Moore. He wanted to kill Moore anyway after all; that monster had killed his friends, had threatened his allies. He was still himself, he still cared for Ari and ... He grunted as Muneed pushed back against him, a labial tendril wrapping around his testes and squeezing. The message was clear: his job was to fill her with cum, she would kill the upstart male that wanted to interrupt. Dan was in awe of the perfection that was his mate. Sexy, beautiful, virile, violent, perfect in every way. He hissed his assent as he gripped her ass, digging his nails into the meat to guarantee he wouldn't be knocked loose.

Muneed reared back, swiping the air as Moore

came close. He was sluggish, Dan could see that; he had been badly hurt by Jeremy, and now he was full of food too. No matter how badly he wanted to knock Dan loose and have Muneed to himself, he was in no shape to fight. Dan kicked one leg up onto Muneed's thigh, and then the other, lifting himself off the floor but allowing himself the trajectory to continue fucking her. His knees and ankles happily adjusted, rotating in a way that would have terrified him before he understood that all biology was extant simply to facilitate his penetration of Muneed.

+

Freed from having to worry about her paramour coming loose or stopping, Muneed lunged forward, her teeth, long and vicious, snapping closed. She was furious at this terrible-smelling weak male that wanted to interrupt her copulation with Dan. Dan was everything she needed. He was strong and caring, he would fill her at her command, he wanted her, and he would protect her and her young, her eggs. Did she lay eggs? Something in Muneed's head screamed. She was married, she had a husband she loved, she had children. But all she could hear was the grind of Dan's cock ridges scraping against the insides of her vagina, and it was driving her mad with pleasure. Her husband had never given her this, he couldn't, confined as he was to the simple round stick that he had the nerve to call a dick. This was what sex should have always been.

Moore, this monster who had hurt her, who had killed her friends, he thought he could interrupt her, he thought he could take Dan's place with his weak flaccid little penis? She would snort if she wasn't so angry. But she was also hungry. And he had presented himself as a meal. A delicious meal of fresh meat that she just needed to rip apart.

Too late, Moore seemed to realize how much danger he was in as Muneed rose to her full height, a stretched out 6'3" of muscle, easily carrying the thrusting and fucking Dan behind her. She fell on Moore, claws rending and teeth crunching. The creature whined in fear and pain under her as she tore viciously into him. He tried to struggle free, he tried to scamper away, but Muneed wouldn't let him. Her long talons hooked into his flesh and pulled him back under her to continue tearing. She paused, allowing Joseph a few more panted and shallow breaths as darkness and death began to engulf him. She could feel Dan growing frantic behind her; his cock was swelling, his balls were twitching. She fell to all fours, biting into Moore's face and ripping the flesh off of his skull. She felt Dan pound into her and release a torrent of cum into her body. She muffled her screams of pleasure into Joseph's eye socket, feeling his brains jelly under the sonic assault. She didn't care, all she cared about was how full Dan made her feel. He had filled her, and it had been amazing, so much more amazing than any watery cum her frail husband had ever managed. She loved Dan; had she always loved Dan? No, but now she had experienced a real male, and she wouldn't settle for less. They would need to band together, care for one another, to protect their superior genetics.

She tore a great chunk of flesh out of Moore's throat and swallowed the wet raw meat down her throat, another pleasure she had denied herself for far too long. She grunted at Dan; he would need to eat too.

She felt him falling away from her, regaining his footing. She moved aside, giving him access to the still twitching corpse under her. They would regain their energy and fuck again and again, until she was fully fertilized. One of her eyes swiveled back to the man—his name was King, she dimly remembered. He was a threat. She saw Ari too; he was a friend. He was a member of the pod, but he was weak, frail. He reminded her of the prior-husband. Would she get a divorce? The word sounded in her skull, bouncing around through rapidly shifting synapses. No, she didn't need to; if he objected to her new partner, she would kill him.

What about her kids? She considered that for a moment as she reached down to rip one of Moore's arms free and bring the meaty bicep to her mouth. Children, they were part of her pod, but they were older, they were bigger. What if they wanted to eat her eggs, or kill Dan's young to protect their own resources? No, that couldn't be allowed. They were old enough to fend for themselves, to start their own pod. She brought her attention back to Ari; he wasn't strong enough. He was weak.

"Arshi?" she asked Dan, wondering what he would think of keeping another weaker male safe.

Dan glanced up, pulling himself out from Moore's guts, intestines dangling from his mouth. Dan bit through the ropy material, spilling bits of Jeremy that had been in Moore's digestive tract

114

to the floor. He turned his head, looking towards the two men, seeming to consider the unvoiced question from Muneed. With a full stomach and an empty scrotum, he seemed to feel much better. She would maintain that balance. He nodded after several moments, confirming what she had been thinking. Ari was no competition to Dan, but he was pod. Family. Family, pod, pack, unit.

She didn't know what use he would be yet, but he didn't smell like a threat.

She looked back to King; he did smell like a threat. He was stronger than Ari, but he was poisoned. The smell that came off him was sickly and gruesome, like a predator who only went for the weakest and youngest of prey. She rose from Moore's corpse. That person needed to die before he could spread his illness further, before he found some weak or confused female and spread his own genetics. For the good of the species, she would tear him apart.

# Abhorrent Faith

# Chapter 8

Ari watched horrified as his two friends, Muneed and Dan, feasted on the body of Moore. Were they still his friends? They had transformed into hideous monsters, terrifying creatures of claws and teeth and extra limbs. Ari was horrified and felt a deep pit of despair and hopelessness open inside him. What if they were under the control of King too? But if that were the case, why had Jeremy attacked Moore? Why had Muneed murdered Moore? They weren't his friends anymore, but they didn't seem to serve King either. Which meant that King didn't have any power anymore. Ari let out a long breath. He could see Muneed looking at him. He still felt terror, but he was less afraid of the monster Muneed had become than he was of a Christian demanding debate.

"I think it's time for you to go," Ari said to King. He still needed to go help his wife, check on the kids. He was terrified that this was a contagious disease or chemical attack. What if someone upstairs had changed? What if the children were affected? On one hand, the fact that she hadn't come back suggested everything was okay; on the other, it suggested she had gotten hurt or hadn't even made it. Did King have more followers like Moore in the building? Ari was growing more and more agitated; he needed to check on his wife, on the Sunday school kids. He took a step forward.

King growled. His throat was swollen like the deflated neck sack of a bullfrog or an emptied scrotum. It vibrated, the loose folds of skin that had begun under his high collar shirt and tie and now spilled out over his chest, wobbling as the sound rolled up from his chest and past his thin lips. The skin inflated, and Moore's eyes bugged out from the sockets as though the pressure in his skull would burst his head. Slowly, he deflated again. He looked almost entirely human, or at least as human as he had looked when he entered. There was something so terribly off-putting about the man, even when he wasn't inflating himself like a sickly pink bullfrog.

Ari was nervous. What if King displayed the same abnormal strength and monstrous mutations? Was Ari about to commit suicide by trying to get past him? He wasn't sure. But it was now or never. He thought of his wife and the kids who were trapped upstairs. It had only been an hour or so since the nightmare had started, but it felt like eternity. He steeled himself and took another step forward.

King responded by inflating again and bellowing, "You will stop!" The guttural roar, boosted by the inflated neck sack, nearly pushed Ari back; it was a tonal and sonar nightmare that seemed to have mass in its intensity. King panted as if trying to catch his breath, to maintain his humanity. It was obviously a lost cause. He was slipping further towards being the monster he had always been on the inside. "Your demons may have killed one of my angels, but the world is filled with the faithful and the lost, and I will scour you and your sickening breed from the Earth." His mouth, thin-lipped and wide, struggled to pronounce the words around ugly jutting tusks that were emerging from his lower jaw. "All who deny Christ will suffer the wrath of God!" He surged forward, his mouth stretching so much that it looked like he would swallow Ari whole.

A roar sounded from across the auditorium.

Ari looked, his heart sinking as Muneed and Dan, or the things that had once been Muneed and Dad, charged towards him. King swiveled his swelling head towards this new threat and spread his arms wide in challenge. He was making himself look larger, but he was also growing larger. When he had entered the Synagogue, King had been a slight man with a cartoonishly oversized head. Now he was swelling as if his body was trying to catch up. But where Muneed was an armored and muscled monster, King was a blubbery toad. He was big and scrawny all at once. Dan hadn't grown at all, at least not in his frame, the phallus swinging between his legs as he charged Muneed was staggering and alien. The rest of his body seemed to be changing, evolving so that he could better clamp onto Muneed, like a male angler fish.

+

King took a labored step, his knees barely wanting to support his mass as he stalked forward. His clothing ripped at the seams, unable to contain the bloated, shivering flesh beneath. His arms stretched grotesquely as bone talons pushed out from under his nail beds. Ari watched in horror as the two inhuman titans clashed.

King backhanded Muneed as she leapt at him, seemingly without effort. Muneed flew several yards, revealing that the simple swat had terrible power behind it. Muneed tumbled as she landed and rolled back to her feet, a high whine pushing through her lips as she righted herself. Her jaw hung loosely; she reached up with one misshapen hand and snapped it back into place with a terrible crunch.

Dan howled his support of Muneed but did not approach the larger male; instead, he moved beside Ari. He could smell Ari's fear and understood. Dan's genetics were superior to King's, but he wasn't built to fight him. Muneed was, she was the warrior. But if King killed Muneed, Dan and Ari would be next. And Ari couldn't help at all, he was weak, good but weak.

Muneed wasn't going down that easily, though. She charged back in, her eyes, all of them, locked on King's bloated form and gangly arms. When he struck out at her, she dove under the claws and ripped into his chest. His skin was moist and slippery, and her teeth couldn't seem to find purchase, sliding off his flabby pectorals with hardly a scratch to show for the effort. Muneed screamed in frustration, her two tongues lashing out to flick sweat from her eyes before she punched forward with both clawed hands. But still the mucus-covered skin deflected the blows, leaving only thin scratches welling glowing blood from his belly.

King laughed. "The armor of righteousness!" he bellowed, his words barely decipherable through his warped maw. He bit down on Muneed's shoulder, his tusks puncturing her exoskeleton, though his shorter, blunter teeth could do no damage. The tusks pushed through the other side, cracking hardened plates on her back. Muneed roared in pain and scrabbled to try to get away, but King reached around her, his spindly, flabby arms encircling her and holding her tight against his moist, slimy body. He was still trying to speak, trying to proselytize with a mouth full of Muneed, but the words were lost against her chitin plates.

Dan couldn't let his mate be hurt by this lesser male. He launched himself at King's back. The spines on his arms, long and slender like a porcupine's, pierced the pastor's slimy protection and lodged in the fat, allowing Dan to perch there. Positioned on his back, Dan grabbed the base of his cock and swung it like a mace at King's head. Using the massive member as a club would be unthinkable before today, but Dan knew he had an impressive penis and that the hardened cum-scraping ridges would hurt, they wouldn't be hampered by King's mucus membrane. Dan's dick slammed against King's head just behind his shriveled ear, knocking his head sideways and loosening his grip on Muneed.

Dan warbled in victory, releasing his phallic weapon to scratch at King's bulbous eyes. King clamped his eyes down, letting them sink into his skull and sealing them behind his hard eyelids. He reached back and grabbed Dan, flinging the smaller male into a nearby support pillar.

The distraction and loosening of King's bite was enough for Muneed to extract herself. She let out a terrible hiss and slammed her head forward into King, following Dan's example of using blunt force. King crowed in dismay, falling back and swiping his own claws through the air to keep Muneed from getting too close again. Ichor dripped from his nose. As devolved and horrible as he was, it was still obviously Aiden King, just a horrifying iteration of the madman.

Dan rose from his supine position and limped back towards the fight. Something was wrong. Though King smelled like sickness, he was strong, stronger than he should be. Dan paused, glancing between the trembling Ari and the fight that was raging between Muneed and King. Ari could help. Something sparked in Dan's mind. Ari was a capable man; despite his weak and soft body, he could help, and Dan knew how. He turned away from the fight and grabbed Ari by the shoulders. The rabbi shouted in fear, his eyes wide and panicked. Dan shook his head, trying to calm the smaller male down, he wasn't going to kill or eat Ari.

"Shh, shh," Dan growled. Shushing was hard without the lips he had accidentally chewed off while mounting Muneed. "Gun. Run. Get." Dan watched as Ari took on the light of understanding.

The rabbi slowly nodded, his eyes glancing at the door and then at Dan's hands on his shoulders. Dan nodded; this was a plan. Ari would get the gun, come back and kill the sick male, then they could all make their way to safety to protect one another. He released the rabbi and watched as the little man ran for the doors. Dan knew the word gun meant a weapon, something that would put down the disgusting King. He couldn't quite remember what a gun was, but he knew it would help.

As Ari reached the doors and left the room, Dan turned back towards the wrestling titans. They were closely matched. Muneed, a fierce mother and warrior, evolved in direct need to protect her brood. Dan bristled at the idea of the sick male hurting his mate or harming any of his prospective progeny. He roared a challenge, adding his voice to the bedlam of noise. He bristled; his spines, dripping with toxic slime, quivered as he charged into the fray, launching himself at King's side.

+

Ari burst through the doors of the auditorium and into the lobby of the synagogue. There, laying in a jumble of body parts and viscera, were the remains of Jose. The doors to the synagogue hung slightly ajar. A thin tendril of pinkish mist hovered on the floor, pooling in from outside. Ari had half a mind to check outside, but the sounds of the fighting in the auditorium spurred him on towards the maintenance office. He was so focused on the sounds from the fight that he didn't notice the sound of the sirens from outside or the discordant screeching roars or the steady, earth-shaking steps taken by an uncaring god halfway across the city.

He didn't process any of those sounds; his mind was fully focused on getting to his wife. He dashed through the hallways separating the public spaces for community and worship from the administrative side of the synagogue. He hit the maintenance office door with his shoulder, slamming it open; but once he was inside, he realized he had no idea where Jose kept the gun. He cast his eyes around the small room, scanning for any clue. He hated ransacking in here, but Jose was dead and the synagogue was under attack, if this didn't constitute an emergency, then nothing did.

Ari sat down at Jose's desk and checked under the loose stacks of paperwork and maintenance requests. Despite Ari's years as the head rabbi here, he had no real idea about what went into the maintenance of the building. He had always left those details up to the congregation's president, treasurer, and Jose. He felt a twinge of guilt about leaving those things to others, and a twinge of fear. He would need to figure out how to pass on all of these duties to a new maintenance manager. And then he felt a bigger stab of guilt through his heart for thinking about his own hardships when Jose had given his life protecting the synagogue. Jose, Jeremy, Madri, Dan, and Muneed, the loss of life and humanity was staggering.

Ari paused; he could feel his chest tightening, his throat closing up. He wanted to panic and sob, he wanted to lose all composure, but people still needed him. He pulled open desk drawers, finding only supplies and more paperwork. How much paperwork could one man need to hold onto? Frustrated, Ari slammed the drawer closed. If he were Jose, where would he keep a handgun? Ari looked up at the large utility closet that Jose had installed. It was so obvious. Ari stood and ripped one of the doors open. He was rewarded by a collapsing stack of brooms, mops, hammers, and other tools. Ari wanted to scream in frustration, but he was still terrified of more of the mutated people finding him. He swallowed his anger and his fear, pushed aside the fallen brooms, and stood back up. There, on the top shelf of the closet, was the gun case. Thank HaShem.

+

Ari pulled the gun out of the case and sat back down at the desk. He was in a rush, he needed to hurry, but he also knew that if he just grabbed the gun and rushed off down the hall, he would likely not be able to shoot or shoot the wrong person. He spent a few moments looking over the gun, checking the safety, checking the chamber, checking the magazine. Everything looked right. Now he just had to remember the tips and tricks he had gotten at the gun safety class he had taken and his four trips to the shooting range years ago. When he had first moved to Texas, several members of the congregation had insisted on teaching him how to shoot. After all, they said, if you were going to be in Texas, you had to be able to fire a gun.

Ari had relented as part of an effort to forge connections to the local community, and now, he was grateful that he had gone. Though he wished he had kept up with visits to the range.

He held the gun loosely in his hand as he rose and made his way back to the hallway. He noticed immediately that the fog, the pinkish red mist that had been coming in through the front doors, was thicker now, so thick that it nearly obscured the ground. It had a sour smell to it, like rotten eggs left in the park the week after Christians celebrated Easter Sunday. It was thick and hot, almost seeming to have resistance as he moved through it. He tried holding his breath as much as he could; it had to be related to the insanity he had witnessed.

It occurred to Ari that this could be a chemical attack, a psychosis inducing gas that had Americans ripping each other apart. That made so much more sense than any other explanation. Ari didn't believe that his friends were marked by some Christian devil or were becoming demons. No, the rapid mutation and violence he was seeing had to be hallucinations and psychoactive drugs affecting their nervous systems. Ari paused, looking at the gun in his hand. Dan had sent him to get it. Dan had sent him to get this obviously with the intention of him going back and murdering King. Could he do that? Could he take a life? If all of this was hallucinations, then what if King was actually innocent? What if none of this was real? But what if something *was* happening? His first obligation had to be to the children and to his wife, Sara. There was no question about that. With that in mind, Ari rushed through the halls again to reach his wife and children.

The synagogue was divided into three parts: the worship and community area, the administrative department, and the school. The Sunday school classes were in the back, on the second floor of the school. As he neared the door, he slowed to a jog and then stopped. Everything was quiet, at least everything was quiet in the synagogue. Now that he was listening, he could hear the sounds of the sirens and screams from outside the building. And the terrible pounding that reminded Ari of how mortars were portrayed in movies. More than ever, he was convinced this was a chemical attack— that would also explain the riots. The pieces were coming together now.

He put his hands on the doorknob and turned it slowly.

"Sarah?" Ari called, hoping to reassure his wife that it was him coming to the rescue and not some intruder. As soon as he turned the doorknob, though, he was knocked backwards by something slamming the door into his head. The world spun as he struggled to get back up and shake off the sudden confusion.

"Sarah?" he called again, hoping she would come out and everything would be all right.

But it wasn't Sarah that emerged from the classroom. Several grotesque creatures, maddening malformations of children, appeared, their jaws and mandibles clacking as they swarmed at the door. Behind them, Ari caught sight of his wife's face, or the upper half of it, sitting on a table. The jaw had been ripped off, and her throat was nowhere to be seen. Instead, the spinal column hung off the edge of the table, leading to a messy pile of something hidden in the thick red mist.

Ari screamed. He fumbled for the gun, but these were children. What if all of these were just innocent children and everything that he was seeing was a lie? He couldn't shoot children. Ari stood slowly, his eyes peeled to his wife's dead eyes, frozen in terror at the moment of her death. He didn't look as the children approached on clawed paws and unfurled sucking proboscises. He didn't raise the gun, he didn't run.

+

Dan charged through the red mist. It smelled like sickness, but it couldn't be avoided. Ari hadn't come back, which meant he went after his mate instead of coming back to help. Dan wanted to be angry, but he understood it. Not that Sarah could compete with Muneed, but then, Ari couldn't compete with Dan. That's what made it okay to include the two persons in their pack: they wouldn't compete, but they would provide greater strength together. Muneed was silent as she ran slightly behind Dan; she had been hurt by King, she would need to recover. But they had managed to drive off the grotesque and sick male. Just the sight of her running next to him made him stiffen. He considered pulling her aside for a quick fuck but remembered there were predators around. He could smell them, smell their hunger, and hear the buzz of their hunting.

Ahead through the fog, Dan's compound eyes spotted Ari. He was standing there, not even defending himself as a half dozen smaller, younger predators converged on him. That wouldn't do. Dan let out a high-pitched scream and dove into the crowd of children. These were not his young or Ari's young. Dan had no reason not to slaughter them and harvest their bodies for foodstuff. And an incubation chamber. Muneed would need a safe place to deposit her eggs.

Dan moved, swinging with all three of his arms, slashing through limbs and muscle and sinew. He ignored the screams of protest and cries of pain as he pinned one child's face to the floor with a foot and stomped down hard. He was too busy ripping another child's eyes out with his tongue. Each one of them that died under his assault was one less that could threaten Ari or Muneed. Within moments, the weaker youth were all dead, save the largest female of them. She was older and ready to mate. Dan could smell her sex dripping with promise. Aroused by the violent power Dan had displayed, she splayed back, spreading herself with three fingers to offer herself up to him. Dan stared at her inviting vaginal cavity for a moment, only shaking it off when Muneed let out a low warning growl. Dan bent forward, planting his face in the woman's sex, and bit down hard, ripping and pulling, destroying her genitals and thus her genetic threat to Muneed. He swallowed great mouthfuls of her ass, labia, vulva, vagina, all the way down to the female's cervix. He swallowed, relishing the taste.

She was reaching at him, swiping in panicked desperation. Dan ducked under her reach and grabbed her face in two hands, slamming it back down against the floor with a sickening crunch. He repeated the attack three more times, until blood oozed from her head wound and she stopped moving. He hoped she was not dead; he only wanted to destroy her cerebral function. He grabbed her around the waist and dragged her forward as an offering to Muneed.

Muneed lifted the smaller female from Dan's arms and looked over her, noting her wounds and the implication of her mate's actions before nodding approvingly. She barked a command—they may have been words, but she couldn't form them with her mouth anymore—and began to move towards the front of the synagogue, dragging the unconscious female behind her.

Dan didn't need the words; he bent down to check on Ari. The rabbi had collapsed to his knees during the struggle. He wept into his hands, barely able to breathe. Dan was saddened by the sight; Ari was kind, a good people. But now was not time for weakness, now was the time to flee this place before more sickened predators or competitors came. He grabbed Ari, careful to not impale the rabbi on any of his spines, and loped after Muneed, intent on finding a safe place for them to make nest, mate more, and develop their pack.

+

Reverend Aiden King watched from the roof of the building. His flesh was shrinking back to its normal proportions, the blessings of strength and weaponized form that God had gifted him for his showdown with the pagan forces of Satan within the synagogue. He turned his eyes away from the fleeing forms of his prey, no, not prey, enemy. They were his enemy, and as his biology returned to something approaching human, his rage gave way to cold anger. This world belonged to Satan, but Aiden would wrestle it away from him one Christ-denier at a time.

The beast walked the earth; his massive pink head, the color of homosexuals, was visible in the distance, knocking the buildings of downtown San Antonio over. The glowing creature, strange and alien like something raised from the depths of hell's rivers, stalked across the world ready to kill the unfaithful in its path. He could hear the screams of the guilty and the howls of the mark-bearers floating on the wind. They came with the hot air from a city on fire. Everything would be

135

ashes and bone if the true-believers didn't stop the homosexuals and socialist servants of Satan that now stalked the earth. But Aiden was up to the challenge. He had been called to minister to those who were marked, those who truly wished to atone.

He was the general in the army of Christ and would lead these sinners and non-believers to paradise, by force and blood if necessary. He felt the presence of the angel in his heart and mind. The one who had come to him and empowered him to fight the devil in all of his forms. Jesus would be the master of the earth, the ruler of all mankind. But the angel Semyaza had promised that if Aiden did as instructed, if he crushed the servants of evil in all of their forms and led the repentant marked to glory ... then, under Jesus, Aiden would be king.

John Baltisberger

## Afterword

Thank you for reading *Abhorrent Faith*, the second book in the Abhorrent series. If you read *Abhorrent Siren*, you may have been surprised by this book, it may have been confusing or even jarring. I want to talk about why I wrote this book.

When I wrote *Abhorrent Siren*, I wanted to write a kaiju novel that was telling the same sort of story that Gojira was telling. Namely, I wanted to address a huge problem that our society was facing and talk about it using metaphor and analogy with a giant monster. I decided to address the opioid epidemic in America, and I think I successfully pulled that off. I was, and continue to be, immensely happy with the final product. But Siren is a very specific type of kaiju story. It's about society, and it's about a dozen little stories all at once. You have Barbara, Owen, Mark, Lisa, and El Guapo, as well as a few other shorter stories, and they all entwine in different ways and address the core of the sociopolitical issue in their own voice.

But I wanted to tell other forms of kaiju story, and I wanted to use the same event. While Siren takes place over a few days across all of Texas, Faith takes place in one room for almost the entire book and only lasts about one hour. It's meant to feel claustrophobic. It's a spotlight on one group of people, and it's about their individual lives that hang in the balance, while the kaiju is merely something that exists in the background, hardly even seen. Despite the Abhorrent—the name the military gives the monster in Siren—never playing a direct role in Faith, Faith is still definitely a kaiju story. It's just a very tightly focused lens during the Abhorrent Event.

Secondly, I wanted to write another Jewish book. I spent a lot of 2021 writing science fiction divorced from overt Jewish theology and mythology, and I really wanted to get back to that. Not only back to that, but I wanted to loop it into the greater universe I've been building through my books all together. When I first started off, I didn't know how I was going to do that. This book was slow in coming together. My first plan was to have an interfaith group trapped in a synagogue and have them argue and have tensions rise as things progressed.

But something stuck in my mind. Televangelists. Profit mongers who capitalize on tragedy through fear. Realizing that I could really tell a story about people who abuse the worst parts of religion and faith, especially in the face of terror, I considered what would happen if the Abhorrent Event really did occur. What would people like Joel Osteen or Kenneth Copeland do? Joel Osteen, I'm sure, would lock himself in his mega-church fortress and do cocaine until the very moment the creature ripped out his heart. But Kenneth Copeland? Not only is he a thief and a conman, he's a fear monger, a man who gets his power through the destruction of love, comfort, and kindness. Kenneth Copeland would absolutely identify the Abhorrent as the Anti-Christ beast and assume it was summoned because of Democrats or liberals.

So, I began writing this book about what that conversation would be like, what that madness would be like. What that evil would be like.

And then on October 31st 2021, a young man came to my synagogue, doused the front doors with gasoline, and lit it on fire.

You'll notice I lose the kid gloves at some point in this book. It gets angrier, more pointed. I try to rein it in, I really do. But hatred mongers like right wing televangelists are actually monsters in my book. So, I wrote this book modeled after historical debates between Christians and Jewish leaders. These debates would go on for hours, and in the end, unable to convert the Jews to Christianity, they would often end in pogroms. Jews have been scapegoats for a very long time, since the time of Saul of Tarsis. Painted to be the enemy forever more. I'm tired of it, and I wrote this book maybe to strike back a little bit.

And these aren't fresh arguments. I extensively used resource books and study guides. I looked up translations. I want to show you some recommended reading:

- Levine, Samuel. *You Take Jesus, I'll Take God: How to Refute Christian Missionaries*. Hamoroh Press, 1980.

- Winkler, Gershon. *The Judeo-Christian Fiction*. Lulu Enterprises Inc, 2007

- Eilberg-Schwartz, Howard. *The Savage in Judaism*. Indiana University Press, 1990

- Kaplan, Aryeh. *The Real Messiah? A Jewish Response to Missionaries*. Orthodox Union/NCSY, 2013

- *Jewish Study Bible*. Oxford University Press, 2015.

- *The New King James Bible: New Testament*. Nashville, Thomas Nelson, 1982.

Now this reading was compiled with past reading, and as you can probably tell, these books are almost all from a Jewish perspective. If you want to find other perspectives, such as Christian, Buddhist, or Muslim, I heartily encourage it. I also encourage you to not try and argue with me. I said many times throughout the book, I don't feel the need to convert anyone to Judaism, I don't feel the need to convert anyone away from Christianity.

This book is not me going out into the world to try to convince anyone I am right.

"You'll be really angry at Christianity" is something I've told a lot of people who were looking to convert. I stand by that, but this book is self-defense. If I sound angry in it, if you feel I'm being unjust or too unkind, remember that as I was writing this, people hung swastikas over the highways in my city. Not in the past, as I was writing it. Remember that I had to explain to my daughter why a young Christian man had tried to burn down the place I got married, where she was named. I had to explain to my daughter why her teachers keep showing her Christmas movies and asking her what she wants Santa to bring her.

Remember that every day I am surrounded by people who don't understand that Judaism is not just 'pre-Christians' or 'Christianity minus Jesus.' I am angry, I am frustrated, and I hope every ounce of that is visible in this book.

The next book won't be kinder, but it will be different. There's one kind of kaiju story I haven't told yet. The "Versus." That's coming next. And you'll see Aiden King again, because just like the actual person he's based on, he's a cockroach and won't disappear that easily.

# John Baltisberger

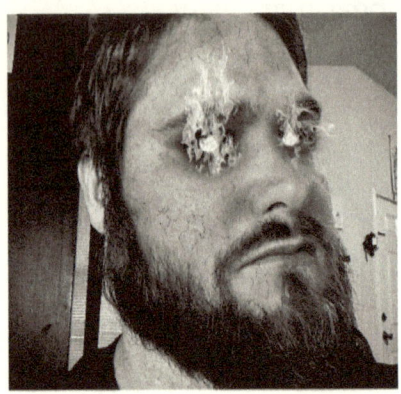

John Baltisberger is an author of speculative and genre fiction that often focuses on Jewish Elements. Through his writing, he has explored themes of mysticism, faith, sin, and personal responsibility. He lives in Austin, TX with his wife and his daughter.

Though mostly known for his bizarre blend of Jewish mysticism and splatter, John defies being labeled under any one genre. His work has spanned extreme horror, urban fantasy, science fiction, cosmic horror, epic verse, and he has even written a guide for mindful meditation. You can see his work and more at www.KaijuPoet.com

# Also Available from St Rooster Books

## From Tim Murr;

*The Gray Man*
978-1799252177
*Lose This Skin; Collectected Short Works 1994-2011*
978-1530351633
*Conspiracy of Birds/Hounds of Doom*
978-1516920631
*City Long Suffering*
978-1519588074
*Motel on Fire; Stories*
978-1543039016
*Neon Sabbath; Stories*
978-1721039708
*My Skull is Full of Black Smoke; Stories*
979-8680276099

## Collection/Various Authors

*To Be One With You; An Anthology of Parasitic Horror*
2018 featuring Paul Kane, Marie O'Regan, Jeffery X
Martin, Peter Oliver Wonder, Adam Millard, DJ Tyrer,
David W Barbee, Ross Peterson
978-1724516787

*Kids of the Black Hole; A Punksploitation Anthology*
featuring Sarah Miner, Chris Hallock, Paul
Lubaczewski, and Jeremy Lowe
978-1072962724

*The Blind Dead Ride Out of Hell; A Literary Tribute to
the Amando de Ossorio Films* featuring Sam Richard,
Heather Drain, Paul Lubaczewski, Mark Zirbel,
Jeremy Lowe, and Jerome Reuter
979-8692365187

Abhorrent Siren by John Baltisberger
978-1-955745-02-4

*Blood & Mud* by John Baltisberger
979-8647568397